Twins of Prey II

~

Homecoming

W.C. Hoffman

Want to stay up to date with W.C. Hoffman and the **Twins of Prey** series?

Join his mailing list and become a "**Twin**."

http://www.wchoffman.com/become-a-twin.html

All "**Twin**s" receive a free short story and discounted prices on future

books.

DEDICATION

To the boys of Lucky Trail and Pine Run.
Thanks for the memories made in the woods.

ACKNOWLEDGMENTS

One of my biggest fans has always been my father Greg Hathaway. Unlike many kids, I did not meet the man I would call dad until I was eight years old. Greg and my mom starting dating and from day one it was never strange to me. We instantly went from something is missing, to a family.

I am so very grateful that as a successful twenty-something-year old single guy who owned his own business, he did not look down upon my mother for having my sister and I. Of course it was not her fault, but it says a lot about Greg that he fell in love with all of us.

As I have grown and become a father myself, I have a greater appreciation of my dad. It is the best job in the world and he has been wonderfully supportive and it also should be mentioned that he is an incredible grandpa. The kids all love their GG.

I remember him saying a few times in my teenage years, "I may not always be happy with you, but I will always be proud of you."
Thanks for always being proud, that meant a lot then and now.

Looking back, I think of all the things he did for me, I hope I am at least half the dad that he didn't have to be.

I love you, Dad.

1 TRUTH

The stage was set inside the high school's gymnasium. Being as small of a town as Pine Run was, this was the largest spot they could use for such an event. Rows and rows of chairs had been placed along the court floor and every bleacher was extended outward in an attempt to fit the maximum occupancy. This was the certainly the biggest event Pine Run had ever hosted. Although it was no cause for celebration.

The number of news crews and camera trucks parked outside was evidence enough that Pine Run would forever be changed. It was not a show or a game that the crowd had arrived for. There was no one famous presenting something or any chance for someone to win anything. The entire population of the small town and the eyes of the rest of the world it seemed had all come to the gym of this tiny American town for the same reason. A funeral.

Along the stage there was not a single casket. It did not make sense to have a casket if there was no body. The front row seating had been saved for the families of the sheriff and his men. For each family held out hope that their loved ones were still just lost out there in the wilderness somewhere. Being that the search parties never found a single body or any signs of their existence the families had no closure. Yet as the months went by each day their hope grew weaker.

Eventually the state police stopped searching and declared the sheriff and his deputies dead. They classified the incident as a training mission gone bad. The news coverage subsided and for a while Pine Run slipped back into a haze of normalcy. With no police force, the residents looked to the state police post that was thirty-five miles away for coverage. Luckily there was very little crime in Pine Run before the entire sheriff's department vanished and that remained true after.

While most people openly talked about what may have happened and speculated wildly, the theories ranged from them simply getting lost, being attacked by a bear, wolves or a lion all the way to them being abducted by aliens. Everyone in the gym had their own idea of what happened to their missing deputies. However, only one person in the room knew the truth.

Henderson's return to Pine Run in the canoe was her secret. Having arrived after midnight, not a single soul was aware she had ever left. Docking the boat inside the Cook Forrest State Park, which was just outside of town, she made her way on foot back to house in the dark, alone.

Waking up the next morning, Henderson carried on as if the entire events of the last few days never happened. Very few knew about the training mission the sheriff was taking the group on. Those that did, had no clue about the sheriff's true intentions. Henderson kept these things in mind as she got dressed for her shift as if it were any other day.

Still racing through her mind was the reality that as far as she knew her coworkers were all dead. Along with her drowned brothers, the world would never know the truth. She felt as if telling the truth would only cause further pain for the families and Pine Run itself. She knew that just the story of them not coming back would be enough to create a media circus. There was no reason to add the story of her brothers onto that. Fueling the fire for the press was not something she was about to do.

Arriving for work that morning she walked into the empty three-room sheriff's department building. The room was just as they had left it. Organized, tidy, and bland. She did the normal things like starting a pot of coffee and sitting down to check the crime logs. If she was going to go on with life as if she wasn't invited to the training mission, then she had to do what she would have on any other day. Grabbing the keys for her patrol car, she walked out to the back lot and after radioing into the River County Central Dispatch to call on duty, she hit the roads. They were not due back into Pine Run for another twenty-four hours. There was nothing to do but to carry on with her shift.

Within a week, the story of the missing deputies was out. Henderson kept up the charade of being the one deputy left behind to watch over the town. It was a believable enough story. She had spun a tale of how they all went camping and planned on practicing wilderness survival and being that she was the girl of the group, she wasn't brought along. Most residents of the town were well aware of how the other others treated Henderson. It was no secret around the barber and coffee shops that she was often the butt end of an offensive joke. If being gay wasn't enough, the color of her skin casted her out just as well. Deputy Annette Henderson was left by the sheriff to look over Pine Run, and that is just what she intended to do.

Lying, she felt was the only recourse she could take. The truth was not an option and throughout the investigation, she remained a rock. Being that interview techniques and mental preparedness where two of her strong points this was easier for her than it would have been for most.

Henderson even assisted with the search parties. These were the times that she questioned her decision the most. While she had no clue on where the twins had fought with the others she did know the location of the underground cabin. Having covered the area many times since she locked them inside its rising waters Henderson ignored it as she walked past the hidden oak door. Paying no attention to it and pretending it did not exist. To her and the others looking in the area the door was nothing more than a piece of an old oak tree.

She rationalized the lies with the fact that she did not kill any of her fellow deputies. In fact she had no proof that any of them were actually dead. Of course in her heart she knew the truth. Yet, this was not a matter of heart. This was a matter of survival. Just as her heart wanted to save her younger twin brothers, drowning them inside the cabin was a matter of survival. Henderson knew the only way she could help Pine Run was by surviving to do so. No bodies, no caskets.

All the lies, all the failed rescue attempts, and useless search parties had led her here to this day. Sitting in the hot gym amongst grieving family members and the intrusive media correspondents. The wives, children, mothers, and fathers of the missing all looked at her asking why she was the one to survive in place of their loved one. Joining them was just about every town resident. School was cancelled and every business had closed their doors for the day. No bodies, no caskets.

Police honor guards from every department in Michigan and many from other nearby states as well as Canada were present, lining the streets of the town with patrol cars as far as they eyes could see. Residents, who could not secure a spot in the gym, lined the streets grasping onto miniature American flags as if they were waiting for a parade to start. No bodies, no caskets.

The groups filed into the hot gymnasium taking their seats one by one.

As time had passed over the months, the reverence for the situation had faded as well. It seemed as if the crowd inside was treating today's event as if it was a celebration of life just as much as they were mourning a loss. Henderson sat there thinking they all should wait until Friday's football game to celebrate something. It also dawned on her that maybe they were not grieving because they didn't know the truth. No bodies, no caskets.

Taking her place in the front row she sat looking at the stage. The podium that stood in the front center was adorned with the Pine Run township seal. Large poster-sized pictures of each deputy were placed on easels that flanked the podium. Amongst the pictures were stands of flowers, each holding a card with a message of condolence for the remaining loved ones. No bodies, no caskets.

As the gym filled with the sound of soulless feel-good symphonic music, Henderson felt the temperature rise as well. It was warm yet for it being early October. Henderson sat there in her dress uniform waiting for the service to start. Unsure if the heat she felt was real or was only due to the feeling of every eye in the room focused on her. As an investigator, she was familiar with the condition called "Survivors Guilt." It was not surviving that she feel guilty about. The lies, all the lies dug into her and made her less of a person. She wondered if this pain would last for the rest of her life and if so, had she really even survived?

Yet she was alive, she had survived. It was now, in these moments, that she realized all of Pine Run was not looking at her with blame in their eyes. Pine Run was looking to her for hope. It was Henderson's job now to protect the town. To heal the wounds her brothers had caused. Without her, Pine Run would be, alone. Thinking to herself, *This is my home and I must protect it, I must rebuild it.* And with these comforting thoughts, the heat was gone.

The service had begun like most others. Being the size that it was, Pine Run only had one church. Father Allen Niko spoke about grace, forgiveness, understanding, and Heaven; all concepts that Henderson was not interested in. Father Niko also talked about moving on and how to do so. Henderson agreed with his sentiments. Of course he had mentioned her in his sermon but that made no difference. Had he only spoken in generalities his words would of affected her in the same light.

The message Father Niko was trying to share with his grieving community were sharp and on point. A gifted speaker originally from the Saginaw area, Niko stood before them a proud black man of considerable size and build. Having successfully grown his congregation throughout his time in Pine Run, Niko was often referred to as the "Cool Preacher" or "The Hip Hop Priest." Both monikers were fitting. While some of the old timers in town could not look past the color of his skin or even his new world ways of spreading the gospel it was the young people Niko was really after. Niko had a gift of speaking to and saving the troubled youth. He truly understood the pulse of today's youth.

Following Father Niko various members of the missing deputies' families took turns speaking. Most of them thanking the community and the other first responders for their diligent work in the investigation and search parties.

Closing out the ceremony was the mayor of Pine Run. A heavy set man in his mid-fifties who always appeared as if whatever he was doing in that minute was the most important task in the world. The mayor in his three piece suit lumbered up the four steps to the stage as if he had previously climbed sixty before reaching these last few. Standing at the podium he reached to pull the wired microphone down to his mouth. The action of his clumsiness with the microphone caused a deafening screech to reverberate throughout the gym. All in attendance gasped covering their ears while shuttering in pain. It was as if someone had drug an entire box full of razors across a classroom chalkboard.

Standing there aware of how annoyed those in front of him were, the mayor looked upon them with a glare of confidence. Being a career politician who had lost his bid as a state representative a few years ago and moved to the town, speeches were no problem for him, normally. The mayor cleared his throat and placed his chubby index finger on the mid brace of this thick black-framed glasses. Due to his heavy perspiration, they had been slipping down his nose from the moment he started climbing the stage steps. Pushing them back up to the bridge of his nose where they belonged, he took a deep breath and wiped away the sweat from where his large white forehead met the black curly hairline.

Having very little contact with the mayor herself, Henderson had no clue as to what the content of his speech would be. She only knew he was close friends with her former boss and that no matter what he had to say or whether or not she agreed with it, this was the man who controlled her fate as a member of the Pine Run Sheriff's Department.

2 SILENCED

"I would like to welcome you all here today. For those of you who do not live in the area or have yet to meet me I am The Mayor of Pine Run. As have the other people who spoke to you on this day from this stage, I too would like to give thanks to everyone in this community. I would also like to give thanks to God for looking over the search crews as they worked so diligently in their attempts to help bring us closure."

The mayor continued on reading from his prepared notes after fixing his falling glasses yet again.

"I would like to say that the sheriff and his men were a great asset to this community. The thin blue line I have come to understand is much like a family crest. It can be dented but never broken. Evidence of that fact stands no more true than in the hundreds of police officer's from around our great state and nation that await you as you leave this gymnasium. We should be thankful for their presence, as they are here to help us in our greatest time of need."

Henderson was sure she was not the only one that noticed the mayor speaking as if he knew the pictured men behind him were indeed dead. Still she gave the mayor credit, thinking at least he had the guts to finally say it. Although this may not have been the best time and place, Henderson felt every person in that vast echo-like room needed to hear it.

"I cannot speak as to the content of the character of each deputy. Mostly so because I did not know them as well as you and it would not be my place. In times like these, as your mayor, I feel it is best to just be strong and a shoulder to cry on if need be. I do not have big shoulders physically but they very absorbent and are available."

Henderson got the picture the mayor was trying to paint even though she thought he was doing a terrible job of it. The perspiration continued growing to a noticeable level upon his hairline of black curlicues that looked like they belonged on a small child rather than a grown man of almost three hundred pounds.

"I can say though what a blessing it was to have our sheriff. I honestly feel that I had the pleasure of working with one of the greatest law enforcement minds in the nation."

At this point the mayor had lost the crowd and even Henderson caught herself rolling her eyes. Anyone who knew the sheriff was aware of his status in the community. This either meant the mayor was as clueless as the sheriff or he was simply lying and trying not to say anything bad about a man whom he believed to be dead. If the residents of Pine Run hadn't already looked down upon their former top lawman before, the fact that he lead almost their entire department into the woods to die did not sway public opinion in his favor. The last thing anyone outside of the sheriff's own family wanted to hear was how great a man he was, Henderson included.

"I think it is important that we move forward from this tragedy and begin to look at law enforcement in Pine Run in a new light. I feel like Pine Run is no longer the small town that no one knows about. I know we have a rich and full history here. Since our founding days life has not been easy for you residents. From the railroad boom in the past all the way through the more recent lumber wars of just decades ago, Pine Run has survived."

Henderson then noticed the mayor had started every statement by saying "I." *For someone in his position it may have been better to talk as a "We,"* she thought.

Typical politician, it is always about him, she said to herself. Henderson sat there eyes open trying her hardest not to roll them again with each point the mayor made. He continued to ramble on and on about how he had hired each deputy and although he did not know them as people he knew them as cops. Henderson got the feeling that the mayor was now off his script as certain parts of his speech had begun to contradict each other. None-the-less she sat there, unconnected not thinking about the true gravity of the situation.

Hot, sweaty and sticky her Kevlar vest clung to both her back as well as her chest. Reaching two fingers down her neckline and under the dress uniform shirt Henderson continually failed at pulling it away from her soaked cotton under shirt, which only provided a mere few seconds of relief until it slunk back down and suctioned itself back against her balmy skin. Henderson knew the people around her had mentally checked out as well as most of the paper programs had been folded and were being used as small hand-powered fans. At least she was not alone in her disdain for the sludge coming from the mouth of the mayor.

Able to ignore almost every word he had said at least was some form of relinquishment from the mind-numbing torture she felt they all were succumbing to. Oblivious to how Henderson felt about his speech the mayor ended it sixteen minutes later with these unexpected words,

"I would now like to welcome Pine Run's new sheriff up to say a few words, Annette Henderson."

The crowd all turned to look at Henderson as if they were unsure of what the proper response was. Clapping did not seem appropriate at a funeral but there were a few who did. The entire room sat there in silence waiting for her to stand up and acknowledge the invitation the mayor had just presented to her.

Only Henderson had no clue as to what they were looking at. Still suffering through her heat-induced daydream, she did hear the mayor's words, but they did not register in her mind as being a part of reality.

"Sheriff Henderson, would you like to say a few words?" The mayor again asked with the intention of getting her on stage to share in the moment. He knew that is was a surprise. Hitting her with the news that she had been promoted as well as asking her to speak when she had nothing prepared was not exactly the ideal situation. The mayor had a flair for the dramatic and anything else full of pompous circumstance. It was almost as if the mayor was setting Henderson up to fail in front of the entire town and all the media present just because it would make for a good show.

Quickly coming to the awkward realization of what was happening, Henderson stood, turned to face the crowd, and nodded. Turning back she walked up the stairs with confidence and met the mayor at the podium. Shaking her hand, he pulled her in close to his chest in what was most likely meant to be a hug but came off more as two football players awkwardly celebrating with a chest bump. Again, the mayor pulled her in close this time with his head almost to her shoulder and whispered into her ear,

"Congratulations Sheriff, don't fuck this up. You know who runs this town right? I do, so don't forget it. Stand up here, look pretty and be the perfect affirmative action poster bitch that I know you can be. It might be best to act like your dead boss and stay out of my way. Those that make noise, will be silenced."

The nature of the threat was not clear to Henderson, but the fact that it was definitely a threat was clear. The mayor let go of her hand leaving it wet and clammy as he waddled his way back down the stage steps taking his place in the front row. Sitting there, he leaned back with a wide grin on his face as if he was watching his master plan of chaos unfold into a perfect downward spiral.

"Hello," Henderson said as she moved the microphone into position once again causing the dreaded screeching sound of feedback reverberating throughout the gym. Visibly annoyed that her speech had started out the same way as the mayor's, she continued on.

"My name is Annette Henderson." The crowd sat still in silence. The mayor had just said her name which was already unnecessary being that everyone in town knew damned well who she was.

Stepping up closer to the microphone she knew this was it, this was her moment. The mayor was right when he said not to fuck it up. Yet taking advice from him at this point did not seem like the best of ideas.

"I wish I could have become your sheriff under different circumstances. I wish I could have earned it. The men who are pictured up here were good men, are good men."

More lies, she thought to herself.

"I came to this department a few years ago and have had the pleasure of serving your community. I have met many of you and for those who I have not, I will." She said beginning to gain more confidence.

"I will be honest with you." She paused.

For once, she thought in silence.

"The mayor has certainly surprised me with this announcement. I had no plans on becoming your new sheriff and I would have hoped there would be a better time than this day to announce it all to you. Having been through what you have, I realize this is not at all ideal. For that reason I will not keep you waiting."

The piercing sharpness of the tone in her voice was not missed by anyone in attendance. Henderson was openly accusing the mayor of being unprofessional. The only question was if he would take it as a joke or if he thought this was a challenge in regards to his *Who runs this town,* comment.

This public revelation did not make the mayor happy. The evidence of that was blatant upon his face. He clearly glared at her through the black-rimmed glasses which again had begun to slide from his nose.

"Although I was not told to be prepared for this, I am looking forward to the opportunity and the challenge. I hope in promoting me we can begin to move forward." Henderson then cleared her throat and leaned in closer to ensure that her next point was clear and concise.

"Mr. Mayor, I sincerely hope that in the future our working relationship is not full of these types of surprises." The crowd smiled in unison and some even chuckled at the idea of her scolding the town's top elected official. The mayor himself did not find any humor in it and only sat there, dead center in the front row looking at her as if in this moment he realized he had made a huge mistake.

"We can do this together. It has been said that it takes a village to raise a child. However I think now and in our future going forward it is extremely important that we…." Henderson paused, "We…." frozen, silent, she squinted and peered at what she was now looking at. Deep into the back of the gymnasium's roofline, something had caught her eye.

There, standing in the skylights that were open to allow what little fresh air there was into the gym, stood two figures; side by side, blacked out by the sun shining down on them from behind. Two dark shapes, equal in size, looking down on her as if they were hawks perched in a tree waiting to attack an unknowing rabbit the entire time.

Be the hawk, not the rabbit, she thought to herself.

Silhouetted in the light, she could not see their faces, but she didn't need to. Henderson knew who was there, above her, watching, listening, waiting. She also knew they must have wanted to be seen by her and only her. For had they just wanted her dead, she would have still been on that stage but only in a picture next to the other deputies.

No bodies, no caskets.

3 HAWK'S NEST

Annette knew that there would always be questions with no answers and that only visiting the watery grave site of her younger brothers would confirm their death. In the time that had passed, she had yet to do so. Even during the search party phases she never got to close to the underground cabin entrance. Her only goal was to keep those in the search parties away from it in hopes of keeping her dead secret alive and well. Keeping the grave unknown was not her only motive.

Henderson simply could not bring herself to visit the place where she murdered her brothers. The act of fratricide was not something she was proud of and her decision to do so haunted her every thought. As a deputy, she had seen over her years what water would do to a decomposing body. Often it was a drowned fisherman or a drunken college kid on a canoe trip that had something go terribly wrong. Seeing her brothers in a likewise condition was not something she was ready to bring herself to do.

The rush surging throughout her body upon seeing both Drake and Tomek perched above her was what puzzled her the most. She had prepared herself to one day go back to the cabin and see their bodies. She knew on that day she would have to be prepared for the grief and to deal with the guilt. One day maybe, but not today. The feeling in her heart was not shock or even guilt. Henderson felt, relief. Full well knowing she may have to kill her brothers again to prolong her own life. She smiled thinking how yesterday she was a murderer, but today she was just a sister. Standing at the podium in front of the most people she had ever spoken to, Henderson kept her cool, thanked everyone in attendance again, and turned the microphone back over to Father Niko.

Taking her place back in the front row, Father Niko's closing remarks fell upon deaf ears. Nothing else in the world mattered except how. How did they survive? How did they get out? Even simpler forms of how questions popped into her mind. Like, how did they get on the roof of the school?

Henderson knew that none of the questions mattered, only the answers. She wanted answers.

The answers to all her questions could have been found right there in Pine Run. Had she known who to ask that is. However, a visit to The Hawk's Nest General Store would have told her all she wanted to know. Simply visiting the store would not help her in finding out the truth, she would have to ask the right question in order to get the right answer.

The Hawk's Nest sat on the corner in downtown Pine Run with the corner of the building only being eighteen inches from the actual roadway. The store's status as a historical building meant common day building codes and sidewalk variances did not apply. The building was there long before those types of laws were written by men in suits and this store was not the kind of place men in suits often visited.

An older building, it had seen its fair share of hard days. The once bright blue paint had faded and peeled back allowing the white primer coat and wood grain to bust its way through. The buildings barn-type style and weathered condition was textbook for vintage. The store was the type of building that would be picked up and placed on a movie set in order to show pioneer days. However this was not a movie set, this was Pine Run.

Stepping into the store, you immediately felt history. The wood floors made from large planks of local pine at the turn of the century shifted and creaked with every step. It was as if dust fell between the cracks of every plank into the basement as you glided across the uneven floor. Every soul that walked in was greeted by the owner's Dachshund pup Sypris as she came barking to the door. Her nail marks ingrained into the wooden floorboards showed her favorite paths throughout the store over the years. The owner would often brag that Sypris was the best tracking dog in Michigan. Most people just laughed it off thinking a wiener dog was good for just one thing, barking. But it often made for a good discussion and more than a few jokes. The basement, that was now a dirt floor stockroom, housed southern slaves in the 1850's who were working their way up to guaranteed freedom in Canada. Having served as a confirmed part of the Underground Railroad meant the building would forever hold its place there on the corner. The Hawk's Nest never did actually see pioneer days, but it did see many a slave during its use as an underground railroad stop as well as many a lumberjack during the mill days.

Metal shelves, electric coolers, and food bins had yet to take the place of all the original hand-built wooded ones that remained in the store. Pictures hung on every inch of every wall. Many documenting the Underground Railroad groups, none of them smiling. Sadly most of those photographs had deteriorated over time and now remained on the wall as faded proof of dark memories. Most of the pictures featured the lumber days and work crews moving massive loads of Northern Michigan lumber towards Chicago. The Hawk's Nest owner, would spin tales to those who asked regaling the glorious lumber boom of years gone by.

The owner's favorite being the story of the great Chicago fire of 1871. The fire had destroyed every inch of almost a four-mile span of what was at that time, the world's greatest city. Michigan, and more specifically northern Michigan became the heart of the rebuilding effort. Chicago was put back on the map one board and plank at a time thanks to the lumber that was harvested here. If not for the fire in Chicago, there would not be a Pine Run.

When the crews arrived at each location to start cutting, certain necessities would need to be made available. These small lumber villages would sprout up and provide all that the hard-working men needed. With Pine Run already having been a stop on the real, above ground railroad that ran from Mackinac to Chicago and then eventually carried on to the Mississippi river, it was in the perfect location. Everything from medical facilities to restaurants littered the villages adjacent to their working areas and Pine Run was no different. As widespread as the industry was, each company had their own way of keeping their men happy. Happy men meant working men. The doctor's kept them healthy while the saloons and brothels kept them happy.

In its life time, The Hawk's Nest General Store had served as a place of business for all those previously mentioned and the owner had the pictures hanging on his walls for proof. The idea of his building having been a one-stop shop for all of a lumberman's needs remained true to this day.

The Hawk's Nest owner stocked everything from groceries to chainsaws and hunting equipment. This truly was where a woodsman would shop. Where a hunter would buy his weapons and ammunition and where a sheriff's deputy like Coleman would stock up on supplies for a training mission in the woods.

All the pictures hung on walls above a small printed out caption of what was depicted except one in particular. The frame stuck out from the wall and was carved from elk antler; with a prominent place behind the register, every customer was almost forced to notice it. There stood two men with their arms upon each other's shoulders. One of the only pictures in the building that featured subjects with smiles. Although he was in the picture, it was the one the owner would never talk about. When asked he would say,

"Every picture in here has a story as does this one. But you see, all the other pictures have stories that are complete. This one has yet to be written."

That was the only thing the owner ever said about the elk antler framed picture of a much younger version of himself and the man. No more, no less.

4 ESCAPE

Taking their last deep breaths from what little air remained in the room, Tomek and Drake both pressed their heads turned sideways against the birch bark white roof of the cabin. Blowing out just as much water from their mouths as the air they took in, the brothers looked at each other.

Throughout their life they both had faced death and escaped enough times to know what it looked like. This time though there was no escape. No air, no life.

"At least we're together," Tomek said laughing inappropriately.

Even with the water closing in the room around them, Drake couldn't help but to find some humor in the fact that Tomek was the one being all sentimental about them dying in each other's presence.

"Yup," Drake replied at a loss for words as they both exhaled mist through their lips and sucked in what might have been their last breath.

As their last drags of air processed through their lungs, the burn of holding onto the carbon dioxide after effects filled their body. Drake sunk down to the floor in the dark feeling it against the bottom of his feet and used what power he had left in his muscles to push off against it rocketing himself upwards to the ceiling in a failed attempt to find air. There was no air pocket to be found as his head slammed against the bark ceiling.

The banging of his head combined with the lack of air left in his blood caused him to suck in a large amount of water. Drake felt the water fill his stomach first and then his lungs. He knew this burning was the last feeling he would ever have. Giving up his fight Drake let his body go limp and begin to sink again accepting the inevitable.

Not expecting to feel anything else, he only felt the life being sucked from his body. Twisting and turning he felt the rush of death as if he was sliding out of the darkness into a white, bright tunnel. Was it the afterlife, was it Heaven or was this his personal Hell?

The feeling was so real, as if his soul had been removed from the pains his body had succumbed to. Drake looked up into the bright light, it hurt his eyes, but it was to glorious to look at none-the-less. Having been so close to death many times in his young life he knew that this time he had actually died. This time was different from all the rest. This time he had gone from darkness to light in just a few seconds. Drake looked deep into the light until it burned his eyes and then blinked.

Why did I blink?

Why is there pain?

He thought to himself.

Drake realized the bright light he continued to stare at was not Heaven or even Hell, it was the sun. Turning his head away from its glare he looked to his right where to his surprise Tomek was standing. Next to Tomek was a dark figure that seemed to be shadowed in the brightness. Drake thought perhaps it was the Devil himself, but as his eyes adjusted to the light he saw a man. A man wearing a full camouflaged ghille suit full of the ferns and grasses that littered their valley. A man with a beard that was clearly white along the edges where the paint that was used to camouflage his face had rubbed off. A man holding a handmade leather-wrapped bow that had a stone-headed arrow adorned to the string.

Tomek was standing next to him as if they had known each other for years. Drake wiped the water away from his face to see that Tomek was standing, with Uncle.

Drake shot up to his knees taking in his first real deep breath since before the water casket closed in on him.

"Uncle?" Drake asked looking at Tomek.

The man took a step forward towards them and quickly answered the biggest question on both of their minds.

"Hello boys, it is good to see you again. You must be hurting and tired. No, I am not your Uncle, but he is my, was my, twin," the man explained.

"The name is Hawkins, most around these parts call me Old Man or Old Man Hawkins or just Hawkins is fine by me," Hawkins said introducing himself formally. Both of the twins sat there looking at the man as if he was Uncle with a different tone of voice.

"I am sure Uncle never explained too much about me to you and that is okay. You see the day he found you, there was a reason he could not just let a set of twins die. He had me and he saw us, in you."

Astonished from both being alive and by the fact that looking into the face of Hawkins was as if they were looking into that of their dead Uncle. However the more he talked, the more they both knew that Hawkins was different than this twin brother. Hawkins spoke with a more educated tone and a much softer voice.

"Quite a pickle you boys have gotten yourself into the past few days, huh?"

"Wait, you have been here the whole time?" Tomek asked.

"Well, I don't know when you all started picking the fights with the sheriff, but as soon as I knew what was happening, I figured I would hold true to my word."

"Your word?" Drake asked.

"That Uncle of yours, you see, many a time, many years ago he saved my ass from, well let's just say much like you I owe my life to him. In return, I told him I would look in on you two after December of last year. Only problem is you guys are not that easy to find." Hawkins said grinning while giving the twins a compliment.

"Tom, um er, I mean your Uncle told me that you guys would be fine on your own, if left alone. Well, when that dipshit jug head Deputy Coleman came in to my store scrounging up camping supplies for the lot of them I knew it was about time for us to meet," Hawkins explained.

"You are a little late don't ya think?" Tomek asked sarcastically.

"Well, hell you must be Tomek," Hawkins answered with a slight chuckle. "And that makes you Drake."

Both boys just stood there in silence, neither one of them in possession of any sort of weapon. Looking at this new acquaintance, it was clear to both of them that he was an outdoorsman. It was clear to both of them that if not for him opening the oak tree door they both would be dead. It was at that point that Drake clearly put together the connection between the feeling he assumed was his soul being ripped from his body and what was actually happening.

Hawkins had gotten the door open releasing the pressure that had built up inside the room. This open portal created an instant geyser which must have sucked their bodies right out of the cabin blowing them into the grassy area below. The cabin expelled them as if they had been swallowed by a whale and shot out it's blow hole. So as Drake thought he was sliding out of his body through a tunnel to the afterlife, he was really just being sucked out of his wet grave into the open.

"Congradu-freaking-lations you know our names, but how are we supposed to trust you?" Again Tomek continued on with his less than tactful conversational ways. "Forget this Drake, let's go find that bitch." Tomek said while turning his back on the both of them and starting to walk away.

"You do realize I could of left your rotten little ass in that hole to die right?" Hawkins asked loudly.

"What do you want, a hero parade?" Tomek replied showing zero respect to the man who was at this point in time just as responsible for him being alive as Uncle was.

Drake grabbing his brother's arm as he passed by him looked at Hawkins and asked, "Again, why should we trust you?"

"Well, that Uncle of yours had just about everything figured out. The only thing he didn't think might happen is this little tiff with our local yokel sheriff department. By the way, nice work with each of them. Well except your sister that is. I figured you couldn't kill her even if you had the chance," Hawkins said.

"Is she...?" Drake interrupted.

"Alive? Your sister? Trustworthy?" Hawkins relaxed his stance and sat down on a piece of log laying his bow on the ground to the side.

"Yes to all three."

With that, both boys dropped their guard as if in some way, without any proof, they knew Uncle's twin was telling the truth. Maybe it was the fact that if a sixty-plus year-old man could track them and the sheriff throughout the wilderness, observe every battle and stay unnoticed the entire time, then the same man could have killed them himself if he had wanted. Any man that could accomplish this type of stealth was either a friend or an enemy of Uncle's and at this point they had no choice but to embrace Hawkins as a friend.

"Now I don't expect you guys to call me Uncle," Hawkins explained. "While we do look the same, I am in no way the same person as he. Just as I am sure you two are very different." Hawkins stopped there expecting a counterpoint from Tomek but the boy remained silent. Hawkins continued, "In time you will come to understand why your Uncle viewed the world in the way that he did. But going forward, you must know that your simple hidden way of life must be put on hold. Your sister is going to need help in the near future."

"We would be dead if that bitch had her own way and now you want us to help her?" Tomek finally broke into the conversation as Hawkins had expected earlier.

"I know and I am sure she had her reasons. Yet I will tell you this, family is the only bond you never choose. It is time to make things right between you all," Hawkins said.

Drake, who had remained silent almost the entire time, looked at Hawkins slowly and deeply. Scanning him from head to toe. Other than being a good amount thinner than Uncle, there was zero doubt in his mind that he was indeed the twin that he claimed to be. However Drake knew there was only one way to be certain. The letter.

"Where is the letter?" Drake asked Hawkins.

Hawkins looked back at him with the same grin that Uncle made when one of the boys had perfected a new skill. The same grin that Uncle made when they first learned to tie their boots, tie a fishing line, filet a bluegill or shoot a deer. The same prideful grin that Uncle was known for was now on the face of Hawkins.

Drake was not the only one to notice it.

"What letter?" Tomek asked.

With that, Hawkins reached into the breast pocket of his camouflaged undercoat and removed an envelope. The back had been sealed with a wax stamp that left the imprint of TH standing. Tom Hawkins, Uncle.

"This letter?" Hawkins said handing it over to Drake. Tomek immediately attempted to snag the parchment from his brother hands but was unsuccessful.

"How did you know he had a letter, Drake?" Tomek asked.

"It seems Uncle shared secrets with us both, you knew of Annette. I knew of this letter." Drake's answer annoyed his brother. Tomek was either unaware of the hypocrisy of his feelings or simply did not care. Either way Drake felt somewhat good now knowing that Uncle trusted him with secrets just as well as his loose cannon of a twin.

"I watched him write it at the table late in the night, before his last trip to town for medicine." Drake explained.

"Yes, that was the last time we spoke. He came to my store sat down and we had a long chat, a few whiskies and hell we even played a little guitar. He left me with the letter and the instructions of delivering it to you this spring." Hawkins said.

"I kept my promise and will continue to do so but for now it is time we head to Pine Run. You can get settled into the loft above the Hawk's Nest and when all is ready we will sit down with that sister of yours. I do not know if I can fix everything that has been done, but I know I can at least keep you all from killing each other."

"The Hawk's Nest?" Drake asked.

"Yes, it is my store and my home." Hawkins replied.

"No, we live here." Tomek defiantly said.

"Look around you, there is no more here for you. You do not have to stay with me but at least come back to my store and see what I have to offer. Plus, clearly Henderson has the drop on you and clearly she does not mind killing you. She is better than you, well trained and much smarter. Your sister is everything you are not, you need her." Hawkins said in a stern convincing matter.

Tomek was hearing the old man talking but was not listening to the content. He thought he knew what was best for him and his brother and right now it was finding their sister and killing her.

"Look here, old man, I came into this world screaming and covered in some bitch's blood. I don't mind going out the same way." Tomek said.

The crassness of Tomek's words raised the eyebrows on Hawkins and for the first time he got a true sense of how damaged of a young man Tomek truly was.

Drake who was now standing behind them both, quietly commented causing both their heads to turn and look at him. There Drake stood with the letter open, dangling at his side as he had just finished reading it.

"We are going with him."

Boys,

This man I have given this letter to is,
Someone I have entrusted to keep you safe.
Always keep a clear mind, trust him. He is my brother.
Love your twin as I do mine.
He won't kill you. He will teach you to thrive.
Learn about him and accept his teachings.
Life changes when you learn.
I kept your lives hidden for protection. I was wrong.
Living in secret was wrong. I am sorry.
My death is not your fault.
Living life out of town is over for you.
Now your return to the old ways can never be.
This is home now, accept the change.
Now go to his home in pine Run.
Forget our woods, there is nothing there now.
Be the snake,
not the mouse.
Be strong,

Uncle

6 TRAFFIC

"Pine Run badge 455 with a traffic stop," Henderson called out to dispatch.

"455 go ahead," replied the county dispatcher.

"I'll be out with a four-door Pontiac Sunfire, metallic green in color occupied two times in the 1500 block of Cole road."

"Break for a plate number," Henderson continued.

"Go ahead with the plate 455."

"Michigan plate, Robert King Larry 8, 3, niner"

"Clear" finished the dispatcher as they begin to run the vehicles information.

Henderson repositioned her spotlight on the back of the suspect car as she exited her patrol vehicle and walked forward towards the driver's side door. While it was not customary for the sheriffs themselves to be working road patrol on a Friday night in a light drizzling rain that was just enough to be annoying, she was the only deputy in town until the mayor gave her the budget to hire more staff. She worked the busiest call hours in an attempt to provide the best service she could to Pine Run. Upon reaching the back of the vehicle, she touched a piece of the green metal just above the left taillight leaving her fingerprints on the vehicle just in case this normal traffic stop for speed turned out to be anything but a simple warning. Ironically it was the former sheriff himself that had taught her that trick. A man who was concerned with her safety more than his own it turned out. Or so it seemed at the time.

Upon reaching the window, she looked inside at the two subjects, both younger teenage black males, close to being juveniles in age. Of course this was not illegal in Pine Run but it was out of the ordinary. "Good evening, I am Sheriff Henderson with the Pine Run Sheriff's Department do you have your license and registration available?" She asked.

The driver who seemed calm and collected simply said "Yes, Officer," while handing the requested identification and paperwork out of the vehicle. She glanced over the young man's license noticing he had just turned eighteen and was registered out of the Detroit area. It was a warmer than normal night and both boys sat there shirtless and sweating as if they had just run for miles. As calm as his voice was, his body told a different story.

"Long way from home tonight aren't you?" She paused to look at the license again and read his name "Mr. Tower, Mr. Lykus Tower?"

"Yes, Officer, I am her visiting my cousin, Jacoby," Tower replied motioning over towards the other subject in the passenger seat.

"Hey, Jacoby, you have any ID on you?" Henderson asked.

"No ma'am,'" he said unwilling to make eye contact staring straight forward into the vehicles black carbon fiber like dash.

"Why is that?" She asked.

"Father Niko takes all that stuff from us when we get to camp and keeps it during our stay," the boy replied.

"Ahh I see, you are one of Niko's boys. Well does he know you are out here away from camp at this time of night?" Henderson asked the still awkwardly acting passenger.

"No ma'am," he replied.

"Then I would guess right about now you are more scared of him than me huh?" Sheriff Henderson joked knowing it was the truth.

"Yes ma'am."

Tower interrupted Henderson's next line of questioning, "What was the reason for you stopping me, Deputy?"

Henderson decided to go ahead and ignore his little power trip game which was an obvious attempt at not letting her speak to Jacoby who belonged back in camp with Father Niko.

"So should I call Father Niko right now and have him come pick you up or, can I trust your so-called cousin here to return you as soon as we finish up?"

"I swear to God we will go right back, I promise I am being totally honest with you," Jacoby said.

"Deputy Henderson," The driver again interrupted.

Not willing to play his game still Henderson quickly corrected him.

"You mean Sheriff Henderson?" She said confirming the driver was aware of exactly who he was speaking with.

"Yea, whatever, Sheriff Henderson," He said while rolling his eyes. "Last I checked this bunghole of a country town is still in America and unless you are arresting me I am free to go correct?"

If the subject matter was not enough then it was certainly Tower's tone of voice which caused Henderson to step back from the vehicle and rest her hand atop of her weapon. Up until this point she had planned on letting them go and following them back to Niko's camp, but now the game plan had significantly changed.

"You are not free to go at this time you are being detained for speeding. Cole road has a fifty-five mph speed limit and I clocked you at sixty-nine just as you passed Lovejoy Road about a quarter mile back. Just wait right here and I will return with your identification and papers in a minute.

Walking backwards the rest of the way to her patrol vehicle she kept her focus on the individuals in the front seat. Knowing that dealing with Niko's boys was never easy but this situation was worse than most.

Father Niko Allen ran his Christian youth camp in the woods on the west end of Pine Run. Originally the grounds had belonged to a bustling summer camp where wealthy parents sent their kids to discover nature so they could live child free for the summer, but as years had gone by and Michigan's economy changed, the camp had fallen on the same hard times as everyone else and was forced to close. Father Niko bought the one-hundred and sixty-three-acre parcel full of numerous out buildings and ponds. The river and cabins transformed the forgotten property into his camp for saving the troubled youth of America. Father Niko never changed the original name of the camp. Lucky Trail had become a significant part of the Pine Run community.

Lucky Trail was a place where troubled young boys could come and live with Father Niko away from their home environments. Throughout their stay they transformed from wild young boys who suffered from a lack of parenting and over all respect for the world into young productive and disciplined men. Almost every child that came into the world of Lucky Trail did so from a history of crime and juvenile delinquency. It was Lucky Trail that took them in, taught them to adapt, taught them to trust in a higher power, and taught them how to become men. Father Niko was often graced with the worst and he turned them, he turned them all. Henderson had thought a few times over the past few weeks that Father Niko and Lucky Trail may have been the only place that could have saved her brothers.

Henderson recognized the passenger in the Pontiac named Jacoby. She had seen him around town working on various service projects that Niko had assigned to him. Pine Run loved having Lucky Trail as part of their community. Father Niko's boys were always around town doing side jobs for free. Community service was part of their mantra. Not an autumn leaf fell in a Pine Run yard that wasn't eventually raked up by one of Niko's boys. Henderson recognized Jacoby which made his level of nervousness seem off putting. That mixed with the reaction of his cousin added to the fact that in her gut, Henderson knew their story was not adding up.

"Dispatch to 455," Henderson jumped a little bit having forgotten she had told them about the traffic stop.

"This is 455 go ahead," the sheriff replied.

"That Sunfire comes back as stolen out of Saginaw County. Taken on today's date at 14:00 hours in a carjacking. Proceed with caution, officer safety warning and I have a Michigan State Police Trooper headed your way. "

"Clear on that, what is the ETA on MSP?" Henderson asked knowing that the closest post was about twenty-three miles away and unless a random Trooper just happened to be in her area she would be waiting quite a while for backup. These backup issues were a direct result of her brothers dismantling her entire department one by one.

"ETA is fifteen minutes, proceeding code one," the dispatcher said confirming Henderson's suspicions on being alone.

"Clear."

Henderson exited the car, this time standing behind the driver's side door as she aimed her drawn pistol at the back of Tower's head. The thin polymer grips dug into her hand much better in the damp drizzle on this weapon versus the last one she had, which was still at the bottom of the river thanks to Drake. Grabbing the patrol car's microphone she cleared her throat, took a deep breath and began to give orders.

"Driver and passenger, put both of your hands out of the windows."

Both occupants did so.

"Driver, with your hands, reach down and open the door from the outside."

Tower again complied.

"Driver, step out of the car and face away from me."

Tower again complied.

"Driver, place your hands on top of your head and interlace your fingers."

Tower again, complied.

"Driver, begin walking backwards towards the sound of my voice with your hands remaining on top of your head."

Tower this time remained motionless standing there looking into the car. Looking directly at the boy he claimed to be his cousin. Ignoring Henderson's clearly demanding instructions.

"Driver, begin walking backwards towards the sound of my voice with your hands remaining on top of your head."

Henderson repeated now lowering her aim to the center mass area of the shirtless young man's body. It was the first time she had drawn and pointed a loaded weapon at someone since her time in the cabin, alone with her former boss. This time her demands did not fall upon deaf ears as Tower took his first step back.

"Keep walking, towards the sound of my voice," Henderson again demanded through the loudspeaker which made her voice echo against the trees and woods that bordered the dirt section of Cole Road where they remained stopped.

Tower took another step before coming to a complete stop. Only this would be the last step backward that he would take. Lowering his right hand to the front buckle area of his pants caused Henderson to demand his hands return to the top of his head.

"Put your hands back on top of your head, I will not ask you again!"

"Don't shoot me I have to scratch my nuts, they itch really bad."

"Hands up!" She replied.

"Come on bitch, you ain't got a set so you don't know."

"Put your goddamned hand on top of your fucking head, now!" If Tower had not taken the tone Henderson's voice as being serious before, now there was no doubt.

"I thought you said you weren't gonna ask me to do that again?" Tower replied as he swung a small .22 caliber pistol out from his pubic line and began running forward. Henderson swung the patrol car door to the side around her hip and pushed off against the dirt road with all the traction her duty boot's rubber sole could muster. Exploding towards her fleeing subject as if she was an Olympic sprinter Henderson closed the distance between her and Tower within a few steps.

The down side of her adrenaline-pumped takeoff was the clumsiness of her gun belt dragging against the side of the car, bumping her spotlight's aim into the sky and off of the stolen car ahead. As she headed towards the Sunfire, she was only guided by the illumination that her headlights provided from behind. At this point the fact that the fleeing shirtless man had a gun was still unknown to her.

The short pop-cracking sound of the .22 pistol being discharged was barely audible over the noise of Henderson calling out the foot pursuit over the radio. Her shoulder mic still being tied into both the dispatch center and her vehicles loudspeaker caused her to hear a slight delay and her own voice over the radio. As drowned out as the sound was, the bright flash that erupted from the short barrel made up for it in the dim night. Tower had never turned to shoot at her as he ran forward but trained the barrel of his weapon towards Jacoby still seated in the passenger seat. Tower had pulled the trigger while simultaneously jumping over the V-area where his stolen car's door met the frame. Showing Henderson she was not the only supposed Olympic athlete tonight on that dirt road, thus using the door as a shield for his body as he continued sprinting into the woods. Henderson may have had him in the sprint, but she never expected to be racing after a hurdler.

The car door shield proved to be effective as it absorbed two of the .40 caliber return fire rounds that Henderson had sent down range. However it was the third trigger pull that found its target. Henderson watched Tower drop with the impact against the back of his body, but had no idea where the round had struck him. The wound's location was evident though as Tower regained his balance and continued running into the woods with blood pouring down his naked back from the area where his left shoulder met the neckline. His blood mixed with the sweat, glistened against the skin in the reflections of the red and blue lights with each flash from the top of her patrol car's roof.

Sheriff Henderson fired two more rounds upon reaching the Sunfire's open driver side door at Tower as he vaporized into the darkness. Neither of them she expected to strike her intended target but it kept him moving away from her which was her motivation in order to check on Jacoby. Just as quick as the traffic stop had turned into a gun fight the mission was now about saving a life, not taking one.

7 MESSAGE

Henderson reached across the front seats interior to check the pulse on the boy she knew as Jacoby. It was there but hardly registered against her fingers. Going around to the other side of the vehicle was not an option for that would not give her any cover in case Tower was just inside the wood line waiting for an open shot at her. She removed the tactical knife kept in the laces of her right duty boot and cut through the seat belt which was the only thing keeping the boys slumping body from falling flat against the dash.

Grabbing onto his shorts at the belt line she pulled him across the open front seat and out onto the packed-dirt roadway. Just as she got Jacoby settled onto the hard ground, she looked up to see another set of flashing lights arrive. This car only had one single red beacon light fixed atop its roof. It was clear as could be in the dark night air that her help was now there. An MSP trooper had arrived.

Trooper Common was a welcome sight to Annette. Having being assigned to cover a multicounty area that included Pine Run meant that Common and Henderson had been on multiple calls with each other over the years. Common was a former minor league hockey player from the Toronto area who had hung up his skates for a career in law enforcement after a series of injuries. Exiting his cruiser he rushed to Henderson's side. The tall and well-built man proudly wore his Trooper-style crowned hat which gave him a few more perceived inches in height. Trooper Common was the poster child for what a Michigan State Trooper should look like, literally. The state often used his image when it came to marketing materials and his face could be seen all over the state on multiple bill boards. Trooper Common was a bit of a local celebrity.

"Is he a K?" Trooper Common said asking if the boy had been killed.

"Negative, but he is not the shooter there is one more. Left on foot into the woods. I think I hit him, at least once but I lost him in the dark." Henderson replied.

"Just watch my back until rescue gets here," she asked.

Trooper Common got back into his vehicle positioning the headlights and every adjustable spot beam he had onto the woods. Soon the front edge of the woods was lit up like a grocery store parking lot. If Tower was coming back they would see him without an issue.

"Annette, rescue is here," Common said motioning down the road.

The ambulance rig pulled up to the side of the road and the EMT riding shotgun hopped out walking towards Henderson who was there still trying to get Jacoby's heart started again with multiple breaths and thrusts against the boys rib cage.

"Trooper Common shining for deer again?" the EMT asked in regards the illuminated woods.

"Negative Kayce," the Trooper responded.

"You guys know each other I take it?" Henderson asked in between chest compressions.

"Yea, he is my brother-in-law," Kayce responded. And then got down to business, "What do we got?"

Unimpressed with the fact that the Trooper's sister-in-law was also there, Henderson gave her the rundown.

"Juvenile male with a gunshot wound to the head. He had a weak pulse which is now gone. He is all yours I tried what I could."

"Thank you, sheriff, we will take it from here," Kayce said while loading Jacoby's lifeless body on the stretcher with her partner. They wheeled the young man into the rear in order to finish the bagging and tagging process from within the safety of their rigs back cabin.

With Jacoby's blood stained across her tan uniform Henderson looked at Trooper Common while opening the trunk of her car and removing the buckshot loaded 1973 Mossberg 500 20-gauge shotgun. A gun that was special to her as it had belonged to her grandmother years ago. This gun had a history of its own. Many a deer, rabbit, and squirrel had fallen from its barrel. The gun even had served useful against more than a few intruders in the night that had been sent off running from the unmistakable sound of its action racking a shell into the chamber.

Henderson loaded shell after shell into the weapon. Pressing her thumb against the cold brass of each round, feeling the pressure of the barrel tub magazine's spring grow with every ounce of lead she loaded.

"Let's go hunting," Henderson said with a half-cocked smile .

"Yes ma'am!" Trooper Common said with the sling of an assault rifle of his own slung over his right shoulder draping the weapon across his chest.

"You ready, Rambo?" Henderson asked half joking at the

impressive amount of firepower Common was carrying into the woods versus her grandmother's old trusty shotty.

"That's how we do it in Toronto," Common said making Henderson smile knowing that was his smartass answer to almost everything.

As they left the bright comfort of their lit up position amongst the patrol cars and ambulance rig it was the quietness of the woods that was remarkably present. No radio chatter, no whirling mechanical sound of the lights as they blinked, flashed and rotated. Just silence. Had they not been searching for a wounded murderer, the moment would have been nice. A cool breeze kept the mosquitos down and allowed the croaking of the nearby swamp frogs and frolicking crickets to pierce the silence.

"Blood, smeared here on this leaf," Common said tracking the killer like it was nothing more than a wounded deer.

"Looks like he kept on in that direction," Henderson answered nodding her head deeper into the woods towards the swamp.

"No, the blood is this way I bet, down this trail some more," the Trooper insisted.

"No he went this way," Common said.

"You are wrong," Henderson said trying to end the short debate.

"If the blood says he went this way, then he went this way, follow the evidence, sheriff. How are you so damn sure he went that way? A hunch? I am not going parading through the darkness on your hunch," Common said.

"The blood says he went that way yes, but now he is over

there," Henderson explained.

"What?" The Trooper asked.

"The blood says he went that way yes, but now he is over there," Henderson stated, again.

"I heard you damned well the first time but what I meant is why do you think that?" The Trooper was no longer doubting Henderson, he just was honestly curious.

"Your said you heard me right, well then use that sense of hearing. What do you hear down your trail?" Henderson asked him.

"Frogs," he said.

"Exactly, and what do you hear down my trail?" She asked making her point.

"Nothing," he said catching her drift.

"The frogs shut up when someone or something disturbs them and gets close. We have two trails. Both going into a swamp full of frogs. One of them is silent and that is the one he went down, blood or not," Henderson said this time turning her back on the Trooper and heading slowly down the path of her choice.

"That is one hell of a neat little trick, where did you learn that?" Trooper Common asked.

"That's how we do it in Toronto!" Henderson replied turning the Trooper's own line against him.

"Good answer," said Trooper Common.

Continuing deeper into the swamp, the soaked ground became mushier with each step. Although they were still on a well- matted down game trail, if not for the blood they had again started to pick up both would have turned back at this point and waited for daylight. But they had blood, and blood meant they were getting closer with each soggy step they made across the switch and saw grass that populated the swamp.

Reaching the edge of the wetland area, the officers came to a muddy bank. The blood stopped there as did all other semblances of the track. There were no footprints in the muddy bank or signs of Tower having attempted to climb it. No brush or grass appeared to have been pushed aside or disturbed in any way. The track had just vanished as if into vapor.

Crack, snap...

The both heard the loud sound of the twig breaking as if someone had taken a step on the bank above them and as they swung their weapons up to the edge it was clear as to what had made the noise. There above them, silently perched as if watching everything below unfold before him was the biggest tom turkey either had ever seen and as their barrel mounted flashlights hit his eyes, the tom let out a resounding,

Gobbbblleee, Gobbbbblllllleeee, Gobble.

Henderson and Common both had heard plenty of turkeys gobble in their lifetimes but none from so close. The sound echoed across the swamp's watery baseline filling the entire valley with a chorus of sound. The turkey's shock gobble was met with the cackling of every nearby crow. Swamp wide not a single frog croaked having been sufficiently disturbed and it all returned to silence just as quick as it had arrived. The noise was gone and they were back there in the same spot with no blood, no trail and no clue.

The turkey still remained perched above them on a limb which visibly annoyed Trooper Common.

"Damned stupid-ass turkey scared the shit out of me ha ha," he said chuckling as he bent down grabbing a loose stone from the embankment's dirt wall. Trooper Common then heaved it up at the bird striking it in the chest. The impact of the swamp rock against the hollow-breasted chest cavity knocked the tom from its comfortable roost down to the ground with them.

Suddenly there amongst the wet swamp floor and the two of them was a furious ball of feathered hate. The turkey regained its composure and with its ground-sharpened razor beak he began to pick and strike at both of his human adversaries. Flapping wings and feathers flew as the bird reared up its legs with each jump attempting to gore his way free from the enclosed area utilizing the one-and-a-half-inch spurs he donned as self-defense weapons.

Not wanting to kill what was an innocent bird just trying to sleep, neither of them fired a shot. The close proximity of them all combined with only being able to see the bird amongst the brief flashes of light as they all bounced around made doing so unsafe anyway.

Reaching for the can of OC spray on her duty belt, Henderson flipped the cap and released three short blasts into the night air aimed at where she thought the turkey's head was at the moment. Much to the surprise of both Sheriff Henderson and Trooper Common the spray had hit the intended target and the turkey's attention had shifted off of them as it jumped one last time taking flight only to travel a mere twenty yards before crashing into the tall swamp weeds from its burning disorientation.

Hearing the bird thrashing around away from them was a welcome sound as they both were now wet from having been knocked to the ground by the tom. They each suffered multiple cuts and scratches from where the birds spurs and beak had found its mark on their bodies.

"You okay?" Trooper Common asked.

"Yea, I think so," Henderson said reaching out to his hand which was lowered in an effort to pull her up off her back to regain her footing.

"You're bleeding," Common said pointing to the scarlet red streak across her tan uniform shirt.

Looking down shining her light on her chest it was immediately clear that they needed to refocus after the turkey incident.

"It's from the victim, not me." Henderson said.

Her tone was enough of a reminder for the both of them that somewhere in the woods ahead of them was a murderer with a gun and at this point nothing to lose. They both wiped away what they could of the mud and water and started looking to the bankside for a way up.

Shining her light up the bank again to where the turkey had been, Henderson was caught off guard at what had taken the fowl's place. The fight or flight instinct took over and being that the turkey was the only one who could fly, Henderson's subconscious chose to fight. The trusted twenty gauge's firing pin held true to its maker as the shot rang out, the pump effortlessly slid back echoing another blast into the night.

Henderson never consciously pulled the trigger. Even racking the pump action slide backwards along its metal rockers and then forward again slamming the second shell into the actions chamber was nothing more than pure reactionary instinct.

Yet there she stood, having fired two rounds of buckshot into Tower before Common could reach her and push her off target. Falling into the swamp grass the third shot rang out just as fiercely as the previous two into the side of the embankment.

The trooper stood over her yelling, "He's dead, he's dead Annette. Jesus Christ, the scum bag already killed himself."

Killed himself, she thought in her head but looking up at Tower's lifeless body, she saw clearly what Common was referring to. He was hanging from the limb with some form of rope or twine wrapped around his neck. Noticing his missing shoe, she quickly assumed it was one of his laces that provided the means for making his own noose. This type of attempt was often used at Lucky Trail by kids who had lost hope.

Yet still, Tower hung there, where the turkey was and neither of them could explain how they didn't see him, only chalking it up to the fact that they were focused on the bird.

Tower hung there with the original pistol shot wound that Henderson had inflicted upon him. Tower hung there with multiple new buckshot wounds that expelled no blood proving they had impacted his already lifeless body. Tower hung there, his own shoelace wrapped around his neck but Henderson knew something did not add up.

Why did he hang himself when he still had a loaded gun in his waistline? Why were there no claw marks on his neck from his finger nails digging into his skin as he grasped at the lace clinging on to the last fledging remains of his life. Why was there no blood around the cord on his neck where it cut into the tightness of his skin as it sucked his life away? Why were there no blood vessels popped in his eyes from the pressure of his fall? This was not Henderson's first hanging, but it was the first one where the above evidence was not present.

Sheriff Henderson knew almost immediately that Tower was hung there after he was already dead and it was not her gunshot to the back of his shoulder that killed him. Henderson knew that Tower's body was also not there when they first spotted the turkey, she was sure of it. How it appeared from nowhere was at this point unexplainable.

During the traffic stop she knew that Tower was shirtless with no jewelry. Therefore why now was there a necklace draped over his head. Tower was adorned with a thin strap made of brown soft leather around his neck which hung down to the middle of his chest. The leather at the bottom neatly came together in an artistically woven fashion around a stone arrowhead. One of her brother's stone arrowheads. They were there, in the woods, part of the swamp, among the shadows of the moon's light that probed through the clouds in the night sky, watching her.

And they had just left a clear message.

8 HOME

Sitting in the upstairs apartment in downtown Pine Run having dinner around a table was becoming a common occurrence in the last few weeks for the Twins and Hawkins. Hawkins was impressed with the boys aptitude for learning how to adapt to modern day society. Of course he had yet to let them leave the dusty confines of the home in the daylight, but Hawkins knew that soon their desire to escape would be greater than their will to obey.

"This bird kind of tastes funny," Hawkins said.

"What do you mean, funny?" Tomek said with a smirk while looking at his brother who shared the same facial expression.

"Just weird, like you guys used to much pepper, where did you get it?" Hawkins asked.

"From the woods of course, last night after we went out for a run. What, you don't like my cooking?" Tomek asked.

"Spare me the guilt trip son, I am just saying it is like you gave this gobbler a bath in a pepper mill." Hawkins said.

"Well, killing turkeys in the dark is sometimes more difficult than one might think." Drake said which caused Tomek to giggle.

Old Man Hawkins knowing there was more to the story lowered his voice and said, "Boys?" As he looked back and forth at them.

It was one of those rare moments when they felt as if they were with Uncle again. Being Uncle's twin meant many of the mannerisms and vocal inflections that Hawkins had, matched those of Uncle. Although it was clear that Hawkins was not Uncle every morning as he woke up and grumbled his way down the steps to open the Hawk's Nest General store.

As the owner of the store, Old Man Hawkins was a staple in the community. A civic leader who tried his best to keep Pine Run as he saw best fit. Old Man Hawkins was the anchor in this community. Running his store on tabs and letting people in need walk out with the essentials needed to survive. Payment would come later, sometimes it never came and that was okay with him as well. Being this type of charitable person is what he hoped to pass on to the twins. Uncle had taught them how to survive and kill in the wild. Hawkin's goal was to assimilate them with the people of Pine Run and let them live their lives however they chose after that.

If returning to their woodland way of life was their wishes, then Hawkins would not stand in their way. Yet no matter which choice the twins were to make, one thing had to happen first. Hawkins had to make sure the new sheriff was on board. Convincing Henderson that her brothers should be allowed to join society or leave it in peace would be difficult. He figured his position as the village council president would be a good place to start.

As the president, Hawkins sat one step below the mayor. Being that Hawkins was not too fond of the politician, he lived by the creed of keeping your friends close and your enemies closer. Hawkins knew that if he ever wanted to be the mayor, all he would need to do is drop his name into the running. Hawkins knew the entire town would back him and the current mayor himself was oblivious to that fact. Although being the mayor would give Hawkins political power he preferred to work the back channels and, if anyone needed to fall on a sword, he would be sure that someone else would be first in line.

Uncle could survive in the woods and teach the boys how to do so. Hawkins could survive in the world but had no idea if the twins would follow his path at this late stage in their teenage lives. Again no matter their choice he knew that dealing with Henderson was the only way to guarantee long-term safety for the boys. This left Hawkins with two options. The first being that he could simply kill her and the second being a promotion.

It was Hawkins who pressured the village council and the mayor to place the gold badge onto the chest of Henderson. Hawkins thought that this tactic could and would work in two possible ways. He hoped that Henderson would be so thankful to him that she would heed his wishes in regards to the boys. Either taking them in as her brothers from down state or ignoring them completely. Either was fine with Hawkins.

Or he knew, as the sheriff she would not want the residents of Pine Run to know that her brothers were responsible for the killing of their entire department. Not only that, but the town would also know the truth in regards to her killing the previous sheriff herself. If Pine Run knew that Henderson was hiding the fact that her brothers were the killers, she might as well have died in those woods amongst her fellow deputies. The disgrace would not only drive her out of Pine Run but end her career in law enforcement forever. Not to mention if Hawkins and the mayor pressed the issue, the district attorney would surely press charges against her for obstruction of justice at a minimum. Old Man Hawkins had Henderson right where he wanted her, in his pocket.

"Boys?" Hawkins asked again. Neither of them answered but he continued on anyway. "I just have one question, if there is nothing wrong with the turkey then why won't Sypris eat it?" Hawkins said tossing a leg bone down onto the floor to make his point.

Immediately Sypris ran over picking up the meaty treasure and began devouring it on the spot as if the spoiled pup had not eaten in weeks.

"You were saying?" Drake asked as all three of them burst into a chorus of laughter. Again another thing that didn't happen often in their previous life with Uncle.

"That wolf eats the hair off of every buck's ass she tracks for us. You really think a pepper sprayed turkey is something she is going to pass up?" Tomek said still referring to the small family dog the same way he did Ravizza's K9 unit, Aurora. To him, a dog was a wolf and a wolf was a dog. That is until it was time for bed anyway. It was almost as if Sypris knew Tomek was the one she had to impress the most and it was his bed she curled up in every night. And once the lights were out, her snuggles and wet kisses were a welcome show of affection to Tomek. For the first time in his life, Tomek felt love.

"What was that about pepper spray?" Hawkins asked.

"Trust me you don't want to know," Drake said trying to cover up his brother's mistake.

"Boys this is my house and I demand to know what you have been up to. We don't need no extra attention brought upon you two." Hawkins said attempting to be firm.

"If you ask again, I swear to God I will tell you," Drake replied in a way that was threatening Hawkins with the truth. Something that he may not want to be saddled with anyway.

"Ah, what the hell, just keep your asses away from the cops and don't kill anything that we won't eat," Hawkins said quickly trusting Drake's judgment not to involve him in the obtaining of their turkey dinner. Giving up quickly on the truth was something that the twins quickly learned Hawkins would do. It seemed that old man Hawkins longed to keep them happy and when it came to topics that were confrontational, Hawkins usually bowed down and let the boys have their way.

The Hawkins home was one of love and trust, not survival or death. As much as the boys enjoyed the hours they spent in their woodland gardens, both of them found it nice to run downstairs and into the store if they needed to grab an onion or anything they might be in need of. Hawkins life was a lazy life, but it was a happy life and if they stayed hidden in the upstairs loft, it was a safe life.

A safe life was what everyone had always wanted for the twins, yet for some reason the twins never felt that a safe life was a real life. The only way to have a real life was to live it as they chose. Free from the rules and dogma of society. Tomek and Drake agreed that when changing lives was out of the question, taking them was the answer.

9 COUNCIL

"What do you mean they were both found dead?" The mayor asked Father Niko in the early morning emergency meeting being held in Niko's office at his Lucky Trail parsonage.

"That is what Henderson told me, just last night. That whore sheriff of yours said that Tower shot Jacoby during a traffic stop and then ran into the woods where they found him hanging from his shoelaces," Niko said rolling his eyes while he leaned back in his posh leather chair from behind his large wooden desk.

"They found him? Who is *they*?" The mayor asked.

"Some MSP Trooper named Common," Father Niko said.

"God dammit, not only is this dumb bitch of a sheriff getting in our way and now the Troopers are in on it as well." The mayor replied slamming his hand down on the desk top while standing up to pace the room.

"Hey, hey, hey. First of all, you will not slam your hand on my desk, this is my sanctuary and you will be wise to not forget who got you elected in the first place. Secondly, this is the house of God and we do God's work here so you will never again take his name in vain in this house and you shall repent for the sin in your next confession!" Niko was now preaching to the mayor who wanted nothing to do with it.

"Really? You are going to sit there and preach to me about fucking sins the day after the two goons you sent on a drug run end up dead."

The mayor said reminding Father Niko that he too was acting illegally.

"Drug run, no. Medication delivery for the ill, yes," Farther Niko replied as if he was claiming that the narcotics his goons were running only fell into the hands of the less fortunate who needed them the most. An outlook that he surely did not believe, but it was a reasonable justification in his mind.

"Running these scripts from Canada down to Flint, is that what you call God's work?" The mayor fired back while pushing the glasses on the brim of his nose back up to the bridge as he made his point.

"The Lord works in mysterious ways," Niko said with a devilish grin while rubbing his hands together like a master villain from some sort of super hero move.

"That he does, that he does," said the mayor. "So what now?" he asked.

Father Niko got up from his chair and strolled around the room looking at the different pictures of each saint that adorned his office walls. Saint Vincent, Saint Patrick, Saint Valentine, Saint Michael. Stopping at Saint Michael, Father Niko stared at the painting for a moment. That moment was long enough for an uncomfortable silence to fall upon the room.

"Do you know who this is?" Father Niko pointed at the picture.

"The Pope?" The mayor replied jokingly as he had no clue.

Ignoring the ignorance of the man he shared the room with, Father Niko continued on, "Saint Michael, the patron saint of law enforcement. You see Michael is one of the few who remains the same across most religious beliefs. Why in Judaism, Michael is the protector of Israel. A great prince who arises to protect his people. The Quran speaks of him as an archangel who visits and protects Abraham. And of course we Christians know the truth."

"The truth is made by whoever wins the war, so please spare me your thoughts on what is real and what is a fairytale," The mayor interrupted.

"Funny you should mention war, Mr. Mayor." Father Niko had now taken the picture of Saint Michael down and handed it directly to the mayor as he continued his impromptu sermon.

"Saint Michael is most known for his fight in the book of Revelations with none other than Satan himself. It was known as the war of Heaven. Defeating the dark angel and banishing him to earth as a serpent. He then later again defeats Satan and the fallen angels where they descend into Hell. Michael is quite the man, well angel."

Niko continued on, "Furthermore, in Thessalonians the scripture tells us that, "The Lord himself will descend from heaven with a cry of command, with the voice of an archangel, and with the sound of the trumpet of God."

"You see God only commands his angels to fight and when his Angels do fight it is Michael that they follow. Michael is the one who does God's dirty work."

"What is the point of all this Father?" The mayor asked growing impatient.

"You see, much like God we have some dirty work that needs to be done in order to save the greater good of our, *my* congregation." Niko replied.

"Will you get to the fucking point," The mayor said.

"And much like God, we have our own Michael. Michael has

completed many a task for me over the years and when I send him to war, we win," Niko replied finally vaguely referencing his plan.

"This sheriff you placed in power must be eliminated from the equation. You either have to bring her into the fold like the last one or she needs to end up dead, like the last one," Father Niko said referring to the drug running arrangement he had with the previous man to hold the position of Sheriff.

"If you want to bring her in and include her so our mutual business does not have any more failures, we must make sure she will play ball," Niko said.

"What about Old Man Hawkins?" The mayor asked.

"Yes, I have been thinking about him, I will work something out. I will make it worth his while to not fight us on this." Niko's answer did not please the mayor, but he did trust the priest enough to handle the old man politically.

"If the old man cannot be trusted or you do not think Henderson will go for it, then we send our Michael into war. Simple as that, your thoughts?" Father Niko asked the mayor not really wanting his input but in a fake showing of mutual respect.

"Send Michael, I never wanted to pin a badge on that bitch to begin with, but Hawkins talked me into it. I am not going to lose another forty grand cause she is out doing traffic stops. This ends now!" The mayor said passionately as he slammed the picture of Saint Michael down upon the Father Niko's desk with such force that the resulting wind blew and array of the Father's paperwork airborne.

Niko looked at the papers and shook his head, "Very well, Mr. Mayor. I will prepare my angels for war. Michael and his crew will be sent there Friday night while the rest of Pine Run is at the homecoming football game. They will be at Henderson's house waiting for her shift to end."

"Perfect, you have to deliver the pregame prayer to the team anyway and I will be in the press box with Hawkins. No one will suspect us. Anything you need me to do?" The mayor asked.

Niko sat back down in his chair, leaning back with his hands relaxed, his long black skinny fingers interlaced. It was as if he was playing poker with people's lives and had just been dealt a royal flush.

Eventually Father Niko answered the mayor's question saying, "No, nothing for you to do. Michael and his angels are good at what they do. Just get a sad speech ready for another funeral. The press is going to wonder why you cannot keep cops alive in this town."

10 COMPANY

After a long night and an even longer day, Sheriff Annette Henderson finally arrived home. So tired at this point from the activities of last night as well as the substantial amount of reporting that had to be done, the fact that she had not eaten in almost twenty-four hours had yet to dawn on her. Trudging into the industrial-sized kitchen that fed scores of working men in years past, she opened up the fridge. Luckily she still had half a lunch from the small greasy spoon diner in town that the locals referred to as Shirley's. Henderson knew it would not be a great meal, but at this point all she wanted to do was eat and sleep.

The sheriff lived alone in a home built to house over thirty. The large three-story brick and mortar estate had served as a dormitory for the loggers and railroaders who worked in the nearby forests of decades gone by. While the second and third floor rooms remained empty and had seen better days as time passed by the main floor was sound and it was there she had made her home. Henderson's grandparents on her father's side had owned the house from the day it was built, but Annette was fairly certain that they had never stepped inside. Henderson House may have adorned their name, but it was not the kind of place her family would have likely spent any time.

The Henderson family, and more so their company, simply named The Henderson Company was well known in northern Michigan. They had been a part of every one of the state's large construction programs since the turn of the century. Everything from the building of I-75 to the Mackinac Bridge had The Henderson Company name on it. With The Henderson Company so involved in multiple deforestation projects it was no wonder Uncle fought so hard against their clear cutting near Pine Run. Thanks to Uncle and his sabotage attacks business became too difficult in Pine Run and The Henderson Company moved out. Thus leaving Henderson House abandoned and bare, much like the woodland areas they clear cut without regard to sound environmental practices.

Annette took up residence in the former house director's apartment on the main floor. Opposite of her door was the large dining room that still held the massive banquet tables that sat and fed the army of lumberjacks and railroaders that called Henderson House home. Off of the dining room was the kitchen, adorned in stainless steel appliances that ran from the buildings natural gas lines. Lines that were, of course, installed over all of northern Michigan thanks to The Henderson Company.

A sitting room and a lounge area, complete with modern couches that mixed with the antique elegant furniture and a black baby grand piano made up the rest of the main floor that Annette used regularly. Storage rooms, shower areas and an old dust-covered library filled the basement areas. She did not spend much time down there, the musty smell alone was enough to drive someone with allergies into a sneezing fit.

While the house was over one hundred and thirty years old it still had its charm. She had acquired it from her family with little resistance and having no mortgage allowed her to finance the never-ending restoration projects that were needed. While she was not a professional carpenter, Annette learned as she went and in the few short months the main floor living quarters had been returned to its former lumber and railroad days of yesteryear.

Henderson House was a place to live but due to the size and emptiness is was never "Home." Yes, for now, Annette knew that she was in a good situation and although it lacked modern touch ups, summer and early fall nights spent on the large screened porch made it all worth it.

It truly was the most beautiful spot in Pine Run. The porch's view casted out over the large hill and grass fields which had not been mowed in years and since returned to their natural river grassland state. At the bottom of the hill was the river, the same river that the twins called home, that flowed right through the heart of Henderson's property. If not for the dam and waterfall in town she could have taken the canoe straight to this point without portage but due to the changes in the natural waterways made by The Henderson Company to install a mill and pond in town decades ago, the midnight portage she completed was the only way around the town while on the river.

Sitting on the porch watching the sun fade into the west skyline as it gave way to a collection of orange, purple, and red clouds, Henderson enjoyed her first and last meal of the day. Too tired to think, she drifted off as soon as her plate was empty to the sounds of crickets conducting their nightly symphony of harmonic chirps. This late in October complete darkness had set in by 6:30 PM and the songs of the owls would soon join in as the moon took its grasp on the night. Henderson slept there on the porch, slumped over in her lawn chair. Not dreaming, not worrying, not thinking. Just sleeping, unaware that she was being watched from the field line.

Thirty yards apart, the two identical fully-camouflaged black teens crouched in the weeds. Scouting their next move and watching Henderson just as they had done the last few nights. Gathering intelligence on Henderson was the only goal. Of course they could have killed her on any of the nights, but this trip was different. This was a mission. Not only were they there to take her out, but they wanted to do so while leaving a message for Pine Run.

11 REUNION

The boys made their way out of the tall grass that hid their position just past the old decrepit yard fountain that had gone dry and now stood only to serve as a crumbling bird bath of enormous proportions. Across the mixture of open yard and cement pavers, they stalked up to the screened porch where Sheriff Henderson slept peacefully in the gliding rocking chair that swung back and forth with each passing breeze as if it was a mother and Henderson was the infant being coddled.

The sounds of the warm Michigan fall night were present as if they had been each handpicked and placed there by Mother Nature herself. The crickets chirped, the owls hooted, and the frogs sang their final ballads before the arrival of winter which would end their frolicking ways.

Silently, step by step, the boys made their way closer and closer. It was as if they were African lions about to pounce upon an unsuspecting antelope. The plan of attack had been discussed and set in stone prior to their arrival. This was not a capture mission, they planned to be in and out leave nothing but a dead sheriff behind.

Stepping up on to the concrete step that led up to the side door of the porch, he looked at her. The scent of lavender filled his nostrils. There was none growing wild in the area and he knew that her body was the source. Looking at her asleep, unaware of his presence the smell made his body and mind fill with desires. Desires other than murder. His partner standing behind him was unaware of the thoughts racing through the mind of the young man in front of him.

As he stopped on the second step, he no longer could smell the intoxicating concoction of wild flowers. The lack of wind also meant Henderson was sitting there still, asleep, not moving, not rocking, not knowing. The screen door pushed open with very little effort only catching a bit at the top where the old wood frame had swelled from years of water absorption. Now inside, they both continued the stalking of their prey and in a few short steps they took their places. Moving across the wooden floored room slowly and methodically as to not awaken their prey, the only disturbance they made was to the cricket in the corner who was less than thrilled with their presence ending his song and falling silent in fear.

The plan was to take her out as quietly as possible. No guns, no fights, no wounds that would allow her to scream. Surrounding her, one in front the other in back they lowered a small tight piece of wire round her head where it rested briefly on her neck. The lack of wind meant that there was no cover or reasoning for the weight of the wire to be on her chest. The silence of the cricket had partially awakened Henderson and in an attempt to get comfortable she turned to her side.

The attacker stationed behind the chair sensed her movement and tightened his grip on the wire with both hands pulling it close to him with all of his power. As he did, his fellow stalker pounced on top of Henderson's body to hold her down. Due to her new side position the wire violently slid up her arm where it followed the path of her shoulder blade and up under her ear where it stopped for a brief second only to slice its way through the sheriff's ear lobe and slide over the top of her head.

The back attacker had expected the wire to catch under the chin against the throat where he would provide the strangling tension and was unprepared for it to be free in the air. Much like a contestant in a tug of war contest who is sent flying after his opponent drops the rope the boy lurched back with his hands above his head still clinging to the wire where he blasted into the glass window pane of a half-opened window. The weight of his propelled body was no match for the antique window and it broke into pieces as he fell through it coming to rest on the side of his rib cage lying, draped across the window's sill half inside the dining room and half outside of the house.

As Henderson's eyes opened, she knew the familiar eyes and young black face of the boy on top of her. Though the lions, now in full attack mode wore masks, Henderson knew the face. She flashed back to her time in the river with Drake when they first met and how he had tried to drown her. Again she was on her back, only this time it was not under water. With fear in his eyes, she knew that she would have to end this battle quickly or he would be taking her life. This was not a time when her negotiating skills would be useful. She had no weapons and no help. This was survival, Henderson was again, fighting for her life.

Pinned down, having no sense of balance to throw a punch or attempt to get up she pulled her left arm free of her struggling assailant and reached down to find his crotch. Sliding her hand down between the two of them she grabbed his testicles with all her might and squeezed while pulling with all the power that she could muster. The boy began to howl into the night like a wolf to the moon. Their goal of a silent attack was all but destroyed as he swung furiously pounding her head with strike after strike hoping she would let go of his manhood. With each fist blow to her head and face Henderson's grip grew tighter and tighter until the pounding stopped and he fell backwards to the ground heaving in pain.

Henderson shuffled to her feet to look behind her and saw the first lion still draped across the sill. Awake, yet confused while bleeding from the lacerations the window carved into his head and face, she saw the gun in his hand raising up at her. As if she truly was an antelope victim to their lion attack, Henderson sprung towards the window, bounding through the air with grace as she landed grabbing onto the top of the wooden window frame and slamming it closed as hard as she could. Falling to the ground in the process as her momentum carried her. The triangle-shaped section of glass that had remained intact and in the frame when he went through it, acted as a medieval guillotine as it sliced its way directly through his clothes and into his stomach severing the spinal cord near the tailbone. The razor sharp piece of dagger glass stopped as it came to rest on the bottom of the sill.

With her weight on the top of the window sill, Henderson had just sliced the majority of his body in half with one fell swoop. Blood poured out from the abdomen and the rancid smell of his stomach contents over took the small room. Lion number one laid there motionless, bleeding out in pieces and done.

Henderson looked back to lion number two and saw him starting to stand up. She bent down and picked up the blood drenched gun and demanded he get back down on the ground. Looking back at her and knowing he had lost the fight, the subject compiled and laid down. Keeping the boy at gun point, Henderson reached inside the doorway to the small door side counter top where there was a roll of electrical tape. The black tape would have to do in place of handcuffs and it held perfectly as she officially took the boy into custody while wrapping his hands tightly together.

Flipping the boy over, she looked at him and asked, "How the hell did you survive?" The masked attacker looked back at her in silence.

"Answer me goddammit, how the Hell did you get out of that cave?" Henderson yelled with her nose directly touching his. Still the boy remained silent.

Angry at the lack of cooperative conversation, Henderson reared back and slammed the butt of the pistol into the subjects forehead rendering him unconscious with a mind numbing pistol whip. The blast broke the subjects orbital bone and Henderson knew she had let her emotions take over. Justified or not, for all intent and purpose, she had just struck a handcuffed prisoner. A major violation of the law yet, under the circumstances, she couldn't care less.

Overcoming her rage meant that the curiosity began to grow. She began to remove the subject's mask cause at this point she had no idea which of them was Tomek and which was Drake. She had no feelings either way, in her mind they both were already dead. Killing them had not been easy the first time and this time it proved to be the same, only this time it was not the same.

With the mask removed and the blood wiped from his brow it was clear, while it was teenaged black males that attacked her, these were not her brothers.

12 ANGELS

The doorbell rang as Father Niko's group of angels entered The Hawk's Nest General Store a mere fifteen minutes before Hawkins had planned to close at 9 p.m. The familiar sound of people shuffling in and out of the store over time had made the bell mounted above the door on its frame useless for all intent and purposes. After so many years, Hawkins had grown to ignore it and it only took a few months for Sypris when she was a pup not to run to it barking her head off. Although the little guardian no longer barked she still welcomingly greeted each customer and guest in hopes for a quick petting session or sometimes even a treat.

This time was somehow different. The bell rang and Sypris hopped up from her resting spot on the side of the cash stand. This spot had quickly become her favorite for it was right in front of the air return that provided her with heat in the winter and a cool breeze in the summer. Reaching the door she took one look at the young men walking in and while she didn't bark the low-toned growl that emanated from the deepest part of her loins was enough for Old Man Hawkins to look up from his copy of the local newspaper where he was reading a short article on the previous week's funeral service.

"What the hell old man, is this thing going to bite me?" Michael said as he was the first one in the door.

"Well now, that all depends on how much money you got to spend son," Hawkins replied in a joking tone, but the truth was he was not too keen on having one of Niko's boys in his store, let alone four of them. Hawkins continued, "You see, Sypris here is a pretty damned good judge of character but every now and then she gets one wrong."

"Judge of character, huh? You mean she don't take a liking to black people don't you old man?" The boy known as Gabriel Durgan spoke up basically making a racial issue where there clearly was not one to begin with.

"Nah, I don't think that is it. See she, is a black dog and you guys are always calling each other dawg this and dawg that. So when it comes down to it you guys and Sypris are one in the same. You feel me, dawg?" Again Hawkins' pointed attempt at humor fell upon deaf ears.

"Hilarious, where are your guns at?" Gabriel asked as he walked past Hawkins in a roundabout way in order to avoid passing right next to Sypris.

Rolling his eyes, Hawkins answered him "Right over there, we haven't moved them since you looked at them all last week Gabriel."

"Man, what the fuck? How do you know my mother-fucking name old man?" Gabriel asked while leaning over the counter for a closer look at the merchandise.

"Lucky guess I suppose," Hawkins answered annoyed that the teen was currently greasing up the glass top to the display case with his oily hand prints as he leaned against it. The truth was it was not a guess at all. All four of them were dressed in the exact same outfit. Black shorts made from a durable type of denim material and their dark green Lucky Trail polo shirts that signified they were Niko's kids. Being higher-ranked angels meant that all of them were older and the color of their shirts was different than the normal resident troublemakers of Lucky Trail. Hawkins knew them to be the leaders, much like camp counselors. Only Father Niko never referred to them as counselors, he called them angels and these were his archangels at that.

Not all of the boys were known to Hawkins. He of course knew Michael being that the twenty-something-year-old soft spoken young man was Niko's number two in command. While Hawkins had no clue to the extent that Niko relied on Michael in his illegal operations, it was clear that the young man held a higher rank than the others. When he spoke, they all tended to listen.

Looking at Michael you would not think of him as a typical type of leader. He was of average height and build and showed no violent tendencies. For being one of Niko's, he seemed much better educated than his counterparts and carried himself in a more professional matter overall. As much as Hawkins did not really care for having the four of them shopping in the store, he was glad Michael was one of them present. This meant that the others would be somewhat behaved.

Gabriel Durgan was everything that Michael was not. The man looked to be older than he was due to his full beard of unusual thickness and his overall build. Standing at six-foot tall, the thick and muscular man-child once had a bright future with a full ride football scholarship to become a Michigan State Spartan. Yet, as it often happens with these types of players, Gabriel Durgan was quickly removed from the team and the University as a whole after causing multiple problems in the athletic department.

Gabriel's mouth, combined with his complete lack of respect for any type of authority, meant he was a lost cause as a Spartan from the get go. He had been a part of Father Niko's program at Lucky Trail as a youth and it was Niko who got him in front of the Spartan coaches to begin with. Niko knew that the Spartan football program often ignored their player's pasts and had become a safe haven for thug types who could not get accepted elsewhere. Michigan State was the only place he could have played and Father Niko was well aware of that.

As the angels spread out and shopped amongst themselves in the store, Hawkins walked over to the quietest of the group. Hawkins didn't know him so introducing himself as a way of getting the boy's name was his way of information gathering.

"Howdy, don't seem to have remembered meeting you," Hawkins said as he walked up to the angel standing near a selection of ropes, chains and chainsaws. This boy would have been easy to remember and certainly hard to forget. While there was nothing particularly outstanding about his size or demeanor the young angel sported a short Mohawk hairdo and was covered in tattoos.

No ink graced his neck or face, but what was visible of his arms, legs, and knuckles donned artwork. The eclectic mix of artwork ranged from a helmet-wearing skull to some type of an orange fish and even the likeness of a three-wheeling all-terrain vehicle was present. The letters scribed across his knuckles were unreadable to Hawkins, but what they said was not important. The fact that they existed was enough for the old man to judge him as being troubled. Any young person who could endure that amount of pain was doing so for a reason other than art.

"They call me 'Hawkins' or just 'Old Man'," he said while sticking his hand out and waiting for a response.

70

"DC," the boy replied not offering a return handshake.

"Just DC?" Hawkins asked.

"Yea, just DC." Said the boy who knew what question was coming next as if he had answered it a thousand times before.

"Well, nice to meet you DC, so what does DC...?" Hawkins was in the middle of his question when the boy looked up and interrupted him.

"Douglas Charles, it was my pops name too. So my family called me DC. You need any more of my life story, old man?" DC said asking the question not really wanting an answer.

"Nope, I guess not." He said. "Let me know if there is anything I can help you find," Hawkins halfheartedly commented offering his assistance knowing it would not be needed nor asked for.

Looking around the room, Hawkins could not decide if they were shopping or casing the store for a future afterhours break in. Each angel spread out into a different section as if they had planned exactly what each was supposed to be looking for.

While Michael had lingered about in the knives, Gabriel stood at the gun counter looking annoyed that he could not pick each one up and hold it at his free will due to its being secured. DC walked up and down the aisles of ammunition with a basket loaded with various types of lead. Hand gun ammunition combined with rifle cartridges and even buckshot shotgun loads filled his basket. Hawkins watched as the tattooed boy's arms grabbed each box. DC was not paying attention to price, but he selected each box with caution making sure that they filled a spot on the list he held in his opposite hand.

The last of the angels had headed straight for the back hardware section of the store and was looking at various tools but kept returning to and picking up the reciprocating saws that Hawkins had on display. Aren Brooks was by far the tallest of Niko's angels and was easy to see from the front where Hawkins' stood as the boy towered over the six-foot-tall shelving units.

Another one of Father Niko's star athletes, Brooks also had the opportunity to attend a free trip to college but for some reason never went. Father Niko had arranged for him to swim at a small school located in the thumb of Michigan's lower peninsula. Brooks stood over 6'7" tall and was thin enough to glide through the water with tremendous speed. Father Niko welcomed him back to Lucky Trail where he served not only as an angel but as the facility's life guard covering the pool and beach areas. His black general issue military-style glasses seemed too small for his head but they remained in place with a tethering strap attached to each earpiece. Other than his height, nothing else stuck out about this angel, but Hawkins could tell that of all of them he was the best educated. Maybe it was the glasses or maybe it was because he was the one looking at tools not weapons. Hawkins was not sure, but he had a feeling that Brooks would be the easiest of the four to talk with.

"You finding everything you need son?" Hawkins asked. "You look a little fidgety? You need to go use the bathroom or something?" Hawkins asked as he noticed the boy's high level of discomfort in the room.

"Oh, no thanks, we got Cokes in the car," Brooks answered.

"Huh?" Hawkins shrugged his shoulders while turning his head to the boy unsure of what exactly he had just heard him say while Brooks just stood there with a dazed look in his eyes.

"I said do you need to use the bathroom or is there anything I can help you with," Hawkins spoke slower this time thinking perhaps he had misjudged the boy he was talking to as being the smart one in the group.

"Ha Ha," the boy faked a nervous laugh. "No, I'm good but thanks," Brooks replied awkwardly.

"Alright then, well you let me know if there are any questions I can answer for you," Hawkins again offered his assistance.

"Well yea, um is this a good one?" Brooks asked holding up the black and yellow battery-powered saw.

"Well, that depends on what you are using it for," Hawkins replied. "What do you have in mind?"

Brooks again grew fidgety and turned away from the old man as if he was just going to walk away awkwardly.

"Hey, old man, leave that fool alone and come show me some guns!" Gabriel yelled from across the store. It was times like these that Hawkins wished he had employees to help him in the store. He could not help but think of the irony behind the fact that Tomek and Drake were upstairs watching television or reading while he was down here dealing with a group of misfits that resembled them so much.

Hawkins walked up to the gun counter and while looking at the most annoying of the angels said, "Gabriel, like I've told you in the past, I cannot and will not sell you a gun."

"Yeah old man, why is that?" Gabriel asked already knowing the answer.

"You are a minor," Hawkins reminded him.

"A minor?" Gabriel said while raising just his left eyebrow. "A minor is a musical key, do I look like motherfucking Mozart to you bitch?" Gabriel quipped back causing the other angels to snicker.

"Last week you tried to buy a couple bottles of the wine we sell from the Loud Mouth Winery. I checked your ID then, remember?" Hawkins said as he pointed to the shelf that held the local winemaker's product line.

"That was for sacramental reasons!" The angel claimed laughing.

"Okay, okay, okay, if you choose to flaunt your ignorance further in my store then I am just going to have to throw your ass out on the street," Hawkins said threatening Gabriel.

"Yea okay, old man, you and what Army?"

"Like I said, I cannot, check that, will not, be selling you anything today because you are a minor," Hawkins reaffirmed his stance.

"So you are saying I am a minor?"

"Unless you suddenly turned twenty-one in the last seven days, then yes. You may not be a minor, but you are too young to purchase wine or a firearm in the great state of Michigan," Hawkins replied.

"Let me get this straight, old man, now you are saying I am a minor?" Gabriel asked while attempting to make a point at the same time. "Cause I aren't no damned minor old man. Do you see a shovel in my hands? Am I wearing a light on my forehead? Is my face all cover in coal? Pshh minor my ass, old man, and fuck you, you racist-ass bitch."

"Gabriel!" The voice of Father Niko froze each of the angels in their tracks, but none were as scared in that moment as the foul-mouthed trouble-maker at the gun counter. The sound of Niko yelling had even caught Hawkins off guard as neither he nor Sypris had heard him enter the store.

"Yes Father," he said while turning to face Niko with his head lowered in shame like a dog who had peed on its masters new living room carpet.

74

"You and I need to have a 'come to Jesus' talk, go out to my truck now," Niko said. "The rest of you finish gathering your equipment for the retreat, pay Mr. Hawkins and head back to Lucky Trail. I am disappointed in you all."

"Yes Father," The group answered in unison.

"My apologies, Mr. Hawkins," Father Niko said while opening the door to let Gabriel out of the store.

"Quite alright Father," Hawkins continued, "Say hey, Father, the art student you got over there with all the doodles on his arms has an awful lot of ammo. That okay with you?" Hawkins asked.

"Yes, he has a list made by me. Do not sell him anything not on the list. These angels of mine were to be rewarded with a retreat to go hunting, but now I am reconsidering it. None-the-less yes, it is okay."

"Very well Father, very well," Hawkins said.

"Have a nice evening, Mr. Hawkins, and again sorry for this," Father Niko said while exiting the store, but before he was all the way out, Hawkins pulled him back in with another question.

"Hey Father."

"Yes?" Niko stepped back in the doorway again ringing the bell.

"Out of curiosity, what you guys going hunting for?" Hawkins asked.

"Coyotes, or wolves, or something like that. We are having some issues with them out at Lucky Trail. The darned things keep getting into the chicken pens," Father Niko responded without a pause.

"Very well Father, very well." Hawkins said as Niko left the store.

Upon Niko walking out, the other three angels placed their various assortment of items up on the counter to be rung up. Michael had gathered a few different knives and lengths of rope while Brooks plopped down the same black and yellow reciprocating saw they had discussed earlier. DC's basket of ammo rounded out the evening's merchandise.

"All this for a coyote, huh?" Hawkins asked.

The angels each just stood there, looked at each other and nodded. Michael then stepped forward handing Hawkins the Lucky Trail's credit card and said,

"Yea, coyote hunting, alright. We's got us a bitch to kill."

13 TRUTH

Henderson left the dead teen splayed out in her window sill with the thought process that he is not going anywhere and waking up the medical examiner at this time of night and making him come all the way across the county was not something that had to be done right away. The other attacker was now with her, sitting cuffed next to her desk down at the sheriff's department. Henderson, at her desk, was looking at him pondering who he was and why he had come to attack her. Was it just a home invasion gone wrong, were they going to rape her, rob her, and who sent them? These were just a few of the questions she had planned to get answers to from the boy.

"Okay, we will start with this," she said grabbing the boys hair on the very top of his head lifting it up so he was forced to look her in the eye. "Who are you?"

"James, and I ain't saying shit to you," The boy replied.

"I am willing to bet that if I put you on that polygraph machine right there, that won't be the truth. I bet your name is not even close to James," Henderson said pointing over to the corner of the room.

"Poly what?" James replied.

"Polygraph, you see that machine right over there? It is a lie detector and I am going to use it on you unless you start talking," Henderson said.

"You see this silent game you trying to play, acting all tough and shit don't work in the real world. This is not the movies cause if it was, your

77

little prick of a partner wouldn't be half dead in my kitchen and the other half dead on my patio. Now why do you think you're alive and he is not? Simple reason is this, I have a use for you. I want information from you and if you are not cooperative and truthful, then you will be like your buddy to me, useless and therefore dead." Henderson threats were empty and a one-hundred-percent bluff, but she laid them on the boy so thick hoping that his youth and inexperience in the world would be her best weapon against him.

"Bitch, you ain't gonna kill me now," James said keeping up his cocky attitude.

The next time James opened his eyes, he was on the floor. His vision was slowly clearing from its blurred state as he tasted the metallic warm wetness of blood in his mouth. Feeling around his mouth with his tongue, James discovered the front row of his teeth was gone. As his vision came to, he saw all four of them on the floor in front of him. Henderson had pistol whipped him with the butt end of her gun in her left hand with a backhand motion. He had been unconscious for almost five minutes.

Seeing his blood-covered teeth on the floor, the boy began to panic and attempted to get up on his feet, but with his head still fuzzy from the impact and his hands still secured behind his back, he only stumbled and fell back down after a few feeble attempts. Henderson standing in the corner could not help but laugh as she loaded four pieces of paper into the machine. Each with one word already printed on them.

"Are you ready to talk now?" She asked.

"You crazy bitch, you knocked my teefe out!" James yelled while spitting out the globs of coagulated blood that had accumulated in his mouth and throat while he was out cold.

"Teefe?" Henderson said mocking the boy's inability to pronounce properly due to the condition of his mouth.

"Yea, my teefe!" He said yelling again.

"Here's the deal, you are going to tell the truth and for each time this machine says you're lying, you lose another one of your, as you call them, teefe," Henderson said explaining her plans to make him talk.

"You can't torture me, I am an American I know my rights!" The boy again yelled.

"Your rights?" Henderson shrugged and laughed and thought to herself for a moment she was acting like her old boss the former sheriff. But none-the-less she needed to know more about the motives of her captive subject.

"Let me tell you something here, you attacked me in my house and then, let's just say you attacked me in my office. Both times I got the best of you. And just so you know when it comes down to it, it is my word against yours and you won't be around to testify unless you start talking now," Henderson again bluffed.

"You see, James, if that is your name, you have thirty-two, nope sorry you had thirty-two teeth. For each lie you tell, I am going to remove one with these rusty old pliers here. With four of those pearly whites missing you now have twenty-eight teeth in your mouth. That means twenty-eight more chances for you to lie," Henderson explained to him while she grabbed his arm lifting him up and placing him into a chair next to the machine. Opening up the lid she placed his left hand down on the clear glass screen.

"This machine measures multiple physical and emotional reactions that involuntarily happen in your body as you answer these questions. Do you understand that?" Henderson said holding back her laughter.

"Yea whatever, I get it," James said. "But before we start, I'll tell you the truth my name is really James, but everyone calls me Jimmy Rae. Just please don't take my teefe," the boy pleaded showing Henderson at this point he truly was defeated.

"You keeping your teeth has nothing to do with me, that is all up to you," Henderson replied again smirking.

"What is so goddamned funny?" Jimmy asked.

"You don't spend much time in office buildings do you?" She asked.

"No," he said.

"No what?" She said again grabbing his hair to lift his head.

"No, ma'am" He replied.

"Much better," Henderson said.

"This machine really works right? I mean, what if it thinks I am lying, but I told the truth?" Jimmy asked.

"I am guessing you do not spend much time in offices or at the library, huh?" Henderson returned with the same question she full well knew the answer to. Being that the supposed polygraph lie detecting machine she had Jimmy Rae hooked up to was nothing more than their office copy machine that she previously had loaded papers into that had the words TRUE or LIE preprinted on them. This was also the reason for her muted laughter.

Sheriff Henderson was well aware of the number of broken laws and rights violations she had committed but at this point it was not about having a good prosecution against her attackers. She wanted to know why they chose her. After battling her brothers and then again the traffic stop gone wrong the fact that again she was fighting two black teenage boys in northern Michigan had to be more than coincidental.

"Now we are going to start, first we will try something easy. Just answer yes or no." Henderson still could not believe this was going to work. "Is your name Jimmy Rae?"

"Yes," he answered as Henderson pushed the green button atop the unit initiating the copy sequence. The light moved back and forth as it scanned his hand and a printed piece of paper shot out of the machine showing a silhouetted outline of his hand with the word TRUE across it in bold lettering.

"Very good," Henderson said holding it up to show Jimmy.

"Was your original goal tonight to kill me?" Henderson asked with her next question getting right to the point.

"Yes," He said as he spit out more blood onto the wood paneled floor.

Again Henderson pushed the button to scan his hand. TRUE. The boys reaction to seeing the results let Henderson know that he was telling the truth but it also told her that this was not a soulless killer. For if he was she would have been dead.

"Were you acting on your own accord?" She asked.

"Accord?" He did not understand her question. "Like a Honda Accord?"

"Were you instructed to attack me?" Henderson asked clearing up the confusion.

"No," The boy said again with blood now at a steady drip from his swollen mouth. Henderson watched as the boy lifted his head on his own this time watching the bright green light of the copy machine cross back and forth as if he was waiting to see this answer more than the others.

Henderson knew again by his reaction that he was lying and was glad she had loaded the paper in the machine in perfect order. As she held up the results scan that clearly said LIE he began to squirm and cry.

"No please, no more, I am not lying. Father Niko sent us only to spy on you. The angels were coming later to kill you for what you did to Jacoby and Tower and because you took all his product. You cost Niko a lot of money and he was saying things about you working too hard and not giving us free passes like the last sheriff. B-b-b-b, but my partner, the dead one you cut up, wanted to impress him and the angels and g-g,get you before they did! Please no, it's the truth no don't take any more of my teefe." Jimmy Rae had cracked. It was clear he was not an experienced killer or even a competent thug and certainly not on the same level as one of Niko's angels. An angel would have never given up this info so easily, but none the less Henderson knew this was not going to be the end of her troubles with the boys from Lucky Trail.

Sheriff Henderson knew this was the truth and no matter how much she wished that it wasn't, she was well aware that Father Niko was not the man that he portrayed himself to be. She knew that the large amount of prescription drugs and various weapons she and Trooper Common found in the trunk of the car she pulled over that night would be missed by someone. Perhaps the Canadian cartel or even some dealers down state, but she would have never thought that Pine Run's own Father Niko was the king pin of the operation. Yet now, it began to all make sense. Niko was not in the business of saving these kid's lives. They were merely pawns in his overall game of deceit and corruption.

Securing the boy with his twenty-eight remaining teeth into a holding cell, she headed back to her house. Not yet knowing her full plan of attack or defense at this moment, she had to do something with the body of the other boy. The longer it took Niko to find out about her knowing the details of his planned attack, the better she could prepare.

Henderson figured once home she could gear up for war and go after Niko in the morning. That way if anything else went bad, she only had to call out the medical examiner once to make sure he was bringing enough body bags.

14 DARKNESS

Henderson pulled into her driveway with her headlights off and quietly rolled the patrol vehicle into the parking lot behind the house. She did not often use this back gravel spot much other than when she had a patrol vehicle to hide. Sometimes it was just easier for people not to know she was actually home and not out on the road working. She entered the house through the screened porch where just hours ago she had taken the life of another young boy. Something that was not getting easier to do with each situation. Even though she always convinced herself there was no choice other than using deadly force, it still weighed heavily on her soul.

Stepping into the room she looked down upon him. Most of the blood was still wet and puddled. What had not soaked into the carpet remained there on the dining room tile floor.

Why? The Sheriff thought to herself.

"What went so wrong in your life that killing me to impress a priest seemed like a good idea?" This time she spoke aloud to the dead boy as if he would answer.

Tiptoeing around his sprawled out arm, Henderson was attempting not to contaminate the crime scene. The thought of this made her laugh because there was no actual crime on her part, in her mind.

Walking through the dining room French doors and stepping into the once grand piano living room Henderson was stopped in her tracks. It was not something she saw or even heard but a peculiar smell emanating from throughout the general area. Drawing in a deep breath through her nostrils she attempted to mentally set aside the metallic iron scent of blood. There was something else in the air, something new, a smell that resembled fresh-cut wood. Henderson had been working on the house long enough to know what the sawdust of the house's old wood skeleton smelled like when cut. She also knew that she had not worked on the house in days. She took one more step into the room and immediately knew what it was that had been cut.

Falling into the cellar through a five-foot hole that had been roughly cut through the floor boards and then covered back up with a large area rug Henderson came crashing into the hole with the rug in tow. Slamming down onto the ground with her right arm in a reactionary attempt to break her fall did nothing but hyperextend her arm at the elbow. While it was not broken, it was useless as the pain began radiating upwards from her arm and into her neck. Slightly dazed from her fall she was unsure if her vision was blurred due to hitting her head or if it was purely just a cloudy mixture of sawdust and multiple decades worth of house dust that hung about due to her unexpected decent.

She had not turned a light on upon getting home and in this part of the house there were no windows to allow light from the moon which stood full in the sky. Reaching for her hip, she suddenly remembered that her duty belt was still in her back pack which she was holding onto prior to when she fell. Inside the pack would be her phone, gun, and a flashlight. Rustling around in the dark she was unable to find the bag in the small room that now somehow held her captive. Feeling the dirt floor and mortared field stone wall Henderson knew exactly where she was in the house. The old cellar coal room.

The coal cellar was storage for just that, coal. In Henderson House's fully functioning days, coal was just as abundant as wood and burnt both hotter and longer with less work to heat the house. Feeling around she found the cast iron metal door that led up and out to the back yard, locked. Even if the room was fully lit, getting out of it in this situation would have been impossible. She was locked in the room with only one way out, up. Yet there was no rope and certainly no ladder. Henderson quickly came to terms with the fact that there was no, hope. Reaching around in her pockets with her left hand, she fought back the pain of her dangling right arm that was all but useless due to fall. As she emptied her pockets she knew that there was not much to be found. Car keys, a lighter, and some gum. Hardly enough to use for any type of escape device.

Henderson sat there for a minute trying to deduce exactly what had happened. Had the floor's age finally caught up to itself and just given way? Or perhaps there was something more going on here. Running her fingers across one of the beams that once was part of the floor joist she felt the cut. Smooth and clean with a ruffled burr on the outer edge. The floor did not break due to old age, she had walked directly into a trap. A trap that had been set in her own house.

Sheriff Henderson immediately flashed back to that fateful day on the river where her brothers described to her how each of her fellow deputies had died. Henderson thought of Coleman, at the bottom of a pit, impaled. She immediately knew her brothers had been inside her house and set this trap. It was clear to her that the lack of spikes meant one thing, for some reason they wanted her alive. As much as she was glad to be alive, she could not believe that the same trap that had captured and ultimately killed a bumbling jackass like Coleman was just as effective on her. She felt violated that the twins were in her house but then she remembered another thing Drake had said to her and although she had never heard Uncle's voice herself she did now.

Prey feels the safest in places it knows, Uncle would teach the boys. *Kill him in his home and he will die without knowing.*

Only she was not dead and that meant that so far her brothers had failed to kill her, again.

Taking the lighter out of her pocket she flicked open the silver lid that once was solid brass but had worn over the years of use and rolled her thumb across the striker. She had never been a smoker but always carried a lighter. Not just any lighter but this gold metallic Zippo brand one. It was given to her by an instructor she had in the academy. An old Navy veteran named Don. While Don was not the best teacher in her school, he was her favorite and the feeling was mutual. The click and clacking sound of the brass top as it performed its opening and closing action was soothing to her. The lighter had been a gift and each time she lit it, the smell of its lighter fluid igniting triggered a fond memory. Now was not the time for fond memories, but none-the-less she was glad to have light.

Poking around the room, she took inventory of its contents. Broken wood, her, and the rug was it. Again all hope faded there in the flickering light of the Zippo's flame. Looking up, she thought about the measurements of the house and knew she had fallen through the kitchen and the basement landing in the cellar. She estimated that the fall alone being almost twenty feet could have killed her, but there she was alone and trapped.

The light went out, Henderson shook the lighter hearing plenty of fluid inside the chamber and struck it again successfully only this time there in the light she saw Drake's face. Slamming the top of the lighter shut she hurled herself towards him only to slam into the rock wall of the dugout Michigan cellar. Reaching down, striking the wick and illuminating the small room again she saw that she was again, alone. Drake was not there, Drake was never there. Her mind raced in an attempt to make sense of what was happening to her. Had she died, was this Hell or worse yet Purgatory? Was she crazy, was she seeing things?

With each thought she had, the level of hate grew inside of her. How could they do this to her, how could they have turned her into this? A blundering fool at the bottom of a pit. Her only hope was that bag, her gun, and the phone. Calling for help was the only thing that would save her. Yet she knew as the only cop in town, help was miles away. She had to get the bag.

Looking up, straining her eyes in the flickering light, the shadows made it hard to see what exactly was above her. Yet looking up there was a small tingle of something shining and in the dark, her mind told her that it was the zipper of her bag. While she knew that in the dark your mind can turn a tree stump into a ten-point buck, she had to hope that it was indeed the zipper. And if she was seeing the zipper that meant the bag was on the edge.

The only way to make sure it was indeed the bag was to try and cast the light on it in some way. With no other options Henderson tossed the lit Zippo up in the air through the hole with enough force for it to reach the top. The lighter's path illuminated the walls showing Henderson the entire scale of what she was dealing with. This first toss was nowhere near high enough and it came falling back down to the coal pit. Ignoring the fact that the first attempt did nothing but highlight multiple nails and screws on its way up that could all easily have looked just like the bags zipper, Henderson threw it upward again. Being forced to use her left hand due to the injury on her right meant the tosses were less than accurate; the second one did travel higher than the first, but she was still six feet short of the floor's opening.

The third toss she put all she had into it and the gold lighter shot up the hole flame intact like a rocket headed to space. This attempt had more than enough gusto to reach the top and she watched as the flame confirmed her hopes. It was her bag laying there on the edge. She now just needed to rig up some way of pulling it over the edge. Holding her hand out to catch the lighter as it reached the pinnacle of its upward motion and began to come back down, the light just hung in the air. As if it was floating, as if she were looking into the sky at the sun. Floating there in the air, not going up, not coming down.

Then a darkness passed between her and the floating lighter as she realized what had happened. Someone had caught the lighter in midair. In the darkness there was a hand, but she could not see the face of her capturer. The hand again crossed between her and the light darkening her tunnel and this time the hand closed the lid putting out the small torch she had relied on for the last few minutes. The lighter was the only thing she had that going for her and now it was gone, along with her hope, again.

Sheriff Henderson knew that either Tomek or Drake stood atop her hole only she did not know which one was there or if it was both of them.

All she knew for sure was that, she was not alone.

15 SERMON

"Hello?" Sheriff Henderson said in an inquisitive manor from her position in the coal room. There was no answer.

"Who is up there?" She asked again and still got no response.

Whoever was above her remained silent for another twenty tense seconds that felt like minutes. The silence and darkness was broken by the clicking of the lighter's lid being lifted and the roll being dragged to create the spark that ignited the wick's fuel. This time with the light held up at the top of her living room she would make out the shadow of a figure.

"Just kill me already, if that is what you are here to do, just get it over with you monsters!" Henderson yelled at her brothers.

"We are not monsters," a voice responded. To her surprise and even her dismay it was not the voice of Tomek or Drake. It was a voice she was unfamiliar with and suddenly she was not sure if that meant she should be hopeful or even more afraid.

"Then what are you?" Henderson asked.

"Angels," Michael answered this time. Michael's voice was distinct and memorable. Henderson knew right away who was at the top of the hole. The only thing she didn't know was if they were the ones who made the trap.

"Then help me?" Henderson asked thinking it was worth a shot.

"Thou shall not murder," DC said.

"They attacked me," I had no choice.

"Tower and Jacoby attacked you too I bet didn't they, bitch," Gabriel said spitting down into the darkness of the whole. The foaming wad of saliva found its mark hitting Henderson directly on her cheek.

"I did not kill either one of them and Father Niko knows that," Henderson explained in her defense but through the darkness she knew the angels were not there to hear her side of any story.

"You killed them you lying whore and now you must die." Again Gabriel yelled at her with a particularly venomous like demeanor.

"Oh yea, what happen to thou shall not kill?" She asked.

Brooks had yet to speak but at this point he chimed in, "Exodus 21:14 tells us that if a man kills ones neighbor, so as to kill him craftily, you are to take him even from my altar, that he may die," Brooks continued on, "So you see Father Niko says you must pay for your sins and thus, today, is your judgment day."

"So you are here to judge me then huh?" Henderson yelled back.

"No, we are not. We are here to send you away from this earth so that you may be judged at the gates of Heaven and then sent on to Hell where you belong!" Michael said.

A few minutes passed of silence and all she could hear was the shuffling of feet and quiet talking coming from above. Henderson could tell they were discussing something but had no clue as to what it was. Henderson broke the silence asking,

"What makes you think you won't go to Hell for killing me?"

"First John chapter five verse nineteen," DC answered.

"Oh yea more verses huh what's that one say, thou had a crack whore mother and thus must do as Father Niko says cause I'm a dumb shit ghetto kid that can't think for himself?" Henderson knew verbally assaulting them was not going to get her out of that hole, but she thought if she angered them enough at least they might kill her more quickly.

Brooks again began quoting a verse from first John, "We know that we are from God, and the whole world lies in the power of the evil one."

"And, I am the evil one huh?" She asked.

"One of many," Gabriel answered.

Michael then said, "We are the angels of Lucky Trail. Sent here to serve God's will under the direction of the honorable Father Niko Allen. Guided by the light of Isiah 13:9 which tells us, Behold, the day of the Lord comes, cruel, with wrath and fierce anger, to make the land a desolation and to destroy its sinners from it."

While professing the word of the Bible Michael took pauses for dramatic effect which was clear evidence of his years watching Father Niko do the same while preaching his weekly sermons.

"Get it over with then, come kill the Devil in the pit, you blasphemous heretics!" Henderson yelled back at them and immediately could tell that they did not like being called that and she may have had finally struck a nerve with the four of them.

"Listen bitch, you are a serpent. This ain't no Daniel in the lion's den bullshit. David verses Goliath shall not be comforting to you either. We are not lions and there is no Goliath up here. We are angels so enjoy your hole and shut the hell up." Gabriel's response to being called a heretic was somewhat of a surprise to her.

While she knew the boys of Lucky Trail were raised by Niko she never really expected them to have this much biblical knowledge. While of course Lucky Trail was a church-based camp, most of the members where anything but church-like. Did Niko choose these angels due to their outstanding faith in God or were they the ones just dumb enough to place their faith into Niko himself? Was Niko, in fact, their real God? Either way it did not matter to her as the truth would not alter the direness of her situation.

"You know what really sucks about all this?" Henderson asked.

"What's that?" DC replied.

"Look what you did to my floor, I worked so hard on that room and you messed it all up," Henderson said trying to cope with her status of near death at the hands of a group of young men yet again.

The group just laughed, "Well, you can thank Old Man Hawkins for that. He sold me this saw, which is gonna come in handy when I need to cut your ass up into pieces before tossing you into the river." Brooks revealed the plan going forward and now that she was aware of their intentions she again wished they would just get on with it.

"Hey, it is dusty as shit down here. Will you throw me down a bottle of water or something. If I am going to die anyway at least let me get something to drink," Henderson pleaded in a strong voice.

Again they just laughed.

"Here you go, drink this," Brooks said.

Henderson didn't hear anything other than the angels laughing at what Brooks had said and then she felt it. Warm and wet and falling onto her in a stream. Brooks had begun to relive himself into the hole which made his cohorts laugh widely like a pack of hyenas standing over a freshly-captured antelope on the great plains of the Serengeti. Henderson was their antelope.

The laughing stopped as quickly as it began and she looked up still unable to see anything but darkness. The stream of urine was replaced by a rushing of wind as if some form of a backdraft had caused the air pressure in her tiny hole to change. And then she felt it hit her. Solid and unforgiving. Unable to tell what it was they had dropped on her, she only knew it was large and heavy with an irregular shape. The object had slammed onto her head and flattened her to the ground it seemed all in one motion. Henderson figured at the moment that this was their plan. To drop stuff on her or bury her or something to that manner until she was dead. She pretty much knew none of them were brave enough to enter the hole and take her on themselves. Like they had said, they were angels not lions. She was not dead yet, which meant more would be falling down on top of her.

Digging the heels of her boots into the ground in an attempt to reach the corner of her small prison where she at least could attempt to hide in a corner and protect herself from the direct blows of the next round of falling debris. Curiously Henderson could only hear the angels above yelling or laughing and she couldn't tell which it was. But there were pauses. Henderson House was well built, yet it was an old house and in houses like that you could hear every footstep made on the floors above you. There were plenty of them hustling around at the current moment which meant they must be getting ready to complete their attack.

Reaching back with her hands in the dark she felt the soft skin like texture of an arm, running her hands to the end of the object confirmed her suspicions. Feeling the hand startled her and if she could have stood up at the moment without falling over she would of quite literally jumped. Maybe even high enough to get her out of the hole she thought.

It was then she realized they had drug the body of the boy from the kitchen floor window and tossed it down upon her.

As if getting pissed on wasn't enough, she thought to herself.

Pushing the dead boy's body out of the way she rolled over to her stomach and in doing so she caught a reflective glimpse of something in what little light there was down there. Reaching her hand out she grabbed it and smiled as the coolness of Navy Don's metal lighter against her skin provided a small bit of comfort. Henderson figured when they tossed the kitchen boy's body down they must have accidentally dropped the lighter.

Clicking open the top and striking it to flame her eyes again detonated into pain from the brightness. As the blindness quickly subsided she looked about the room and realized immediately what all the yelling, scuffling and moving about on the floors above her was due to. The light showed her exactly what she needed to see and she gained her strength with a clear enough head to stand up and look directly at the body.

Henderson was shocked to see what had been tossed into her coal room. She had been joined down there not by the kitchen boy she had killed but by an angel. Brooks now laid there in her pit and he laid there dead. At first Henderson figured he must have slipped while pissing down upon her but as she moved the lighter closer to his body she knew that was not the case. Brooks had been shot in the back with a stone-tipped arrow which was now extruding from his chest with a large piece of his heart's ventricle still attached to it. Tomek and Drake had found Henderson House.

Sheriff Henderson reached down grabbing the blood-drenched

cedar shaft of the arrow and pulled it forward to complete it's pass through of Brooks' chest cavity. As the fletching cleared the rest of his chest it made a dragging sound with the release of air as if someone had let the air out of a deflating Mylar balloon. She stepped on the shaft breaking it into a smaller piece that she could attempt to wield as some sort of a knife or mini spear. This way she had some form of a weapon, as at this point she did not know if her brothers were there to save her or complete the task of sending her to Hell.

Either way there was no light at the end of her tunnel, but with her Zippo there was light in the tunnel and she would at least see the attack coming this time. She would not die in the dark, not tonight anyway.

16 WELL

Dropping to the ground to take cover, each of the remaining angels stationed themselves behind some form of furniture. The couch, love seat, and piano had become their bunkers.

"What in the hell was that?" DC asked.

"A fucking arrow came in from through that back screened porch area," Michael replied still in place ducking behind the piano.

"This is bullshit, who uses a bow and arrow and who has the guts to shoot at us?" Gabriel said in an angry manor of disbelief.

"I don't, know but we sure as hell are going to find out," said Michael.

"I'll go check it out, I'm gonna straight up kill this mutha, " DC said.

Michael was surprised by this valiant show of courage and was not sure if DC was being a hero or was just dumb. Either way he was okay with the idea.

"You do that I'll head up stairs and watch from the window as your lookout," Michael replied.

"No, that's a bad idea, we all need to stay together," Gabriel pleaded not wanting to be left alone and showing a chink in his tough guy armored bravado.

All three of them, now on their knees aimed their guns at the back porch not focusing on what was behind them. The quickness and silence of Tomek's approach was all but equal to the stalking of a mountain lion upon an unsuspecting whitetail fawn. The main difference being that the fawn would have a chance to run.

With three bounds from his position around the corner, he now stood directly behind Michael. Being that close to his prey and not striking, he heard Uncle's voice,

Kill when you strike, do not hesitate. The serpent can still bite after you remove his head.

Uncle's lesson was in reference to a time that the boys had a raccoon in a trap and had spent the majority of an afternoon rattling the cage and poking at it with various objects while laughing at the reactions they got from the furiously freighted animal. It was a time when they were still young and although they had been talked to about killing and the importance of taking the life from a living creature, it was not something they had yet to accomplish on their own. This lesson was Uncle's way of teaching them to kill quick and clean. Drake learned this lesson and followed it with pride, Tomek who was much like his brother in some ways, differed in this approach.

Tomek reached down grabbing the hair of Michael and using a flint-napped stone knife and sliced upward from the bottom of the angel's jaw line towards the sky with his other hand. The vicious cut removed the soft cartridge part of the earlobe sending it flinging into the air where Tomek snagged it for a trophy as he ran forward towards the other two leaving Michael screaming in pain, but very much alive. Michael screeched as he fired his rifle into the side wall multiple times causing his partnering angels to duck back into their respective hiding spots.

Henderson still below in the pit quickly extinguished the flame from the lighter upon hearing the commotion and shots being fired. At that moment she had no clue as to what was going on above her but did not want to become a target. Staying alive in the dark was better than being dead in the light.

Before Gabriel and DC could turn to see what had happened behind them, Tomek had run between the two throwing down a homemade grenade-like ball which consisted of a fine ground powder of fermented nutmeg mixed with the dried and crushed up body of a bhut jolokia pepper from their garden. The peppers were known to the boys as scorpion breath peppers and while they were not natural to Michigan they were grown every year in their gardens. Often they would open them up and rub them on branches and rocks in areas that they did not want deer to enter. The high level of capsaicin present in the peppers would drive away anything that came near it. It was the perfect all natural garden protector.

The ingredients of this attack grenade were then wrapped in a wet cheese cloth, dipped in wet riverbank clay which dried into a shell like casing. This allowed them to store the weapon as well as throw it a great distance if need be. Another specialty of Uncle's training, the grenades were usually the twins' best form of bear repellant, but it also worked just the same on unsuspecting humans.

The mystified powder latched onto every bit of moisture in their eyes, mouth, and throat. All three angels grabbed at their throats and eyes as they withered in pain yelling obscenities and waving their guns about the room only to see the shadowy figure of Tomek exit and run through the kitchen escaping out the back door. Gabriel remained on the ground as he had caught the largest amount of the debilitating mixture while DC got to his feet and rushed into the kitchen reaching for the sink to turn on the water.

DC struggled once at the sink to breath and found no relief from the water that would of normally come from the faucet. Only this particular sink was not in operation at the moment as Henderson had yet to fix the plumbing in this side of the house. Turning to the back door he remembered the old well was just outside in a little courtyard near the parking lot. The fieldstone lined well resembled a theme park wishing well meant to collect the quarters of wishers more so than it did a water source but with the burning of every mucus membrane in his head he did not care, DC just wanted water.

Stumbling out the back door, the angel headed straight for the well and once reaching the side wall he dropped to his knees. With his head over the ledge he spit a large amount of saliva and snot that the powder was causing his olfactory senses to create into the darkness of the hole. Hearing the sound of his phlegm splash onto the water below DC grabbed the rope tied bucket next to him and tossed it down.

Only he never heard the bucket make contact with the water as he expected. Turning around to check the rope he wiped his eyes and saw both Tomek and Drake standing there. One of the boys was holding the end of the thin rope just short of where it was tied to the cinder block that acted as the buckets anchor. Unable to see exactly who they were he shook his head again as if he was seeing double.

The shake did little to clear his blurred vision as he reached for the pistol tucked loosely in his waistband. Pulling the small handgun up and pointing it back down towards the house where the twins stood he blinked again and they were gone. Turning back on his hands and knees he looked down into the well and while he could not see the bucket the moon's full reflection gleamed on the water's surface below which motivated him all the more to lift it up. Turning back around to grab the cinder block and pull it closer to the well he figured that would give him the slack needed for the bucket to reach the water.

Again, just as the twins had vanished before him so had the cement block. Looking around, spinning wildly in a circle DC could not tell if he was indeed going crazy or if it was perhaps the Devil himself playing these tricks on him as a test of his faith.

"Jesus Christ be with me, be with me in this momenmmm…" DC said asking for help from the Son of Christ but was unable to finish his reverent plea due to the block's rope now wrapped around his neck. He sprung up to his feet grabbing at his neck and running towards the house only to be yanked off the ground and into the air by Tomek's pulling of the rope backwards. Seeing his feet airborne above his head as his back slammed against the ground DC again began clawing at the rope which was double wrapped around his neck at this point cutting off his air supply.

With his fingernails digging at the rope and penetrating his own skin the neck began to bleed from the multiple puncture wounds he was creating in a failed attempt and catching even the slightest bit of air. Getting back up to his knees he looked up and saw Drake standing there with the cinder block on the edge of the well's rock ledge. DC began running at him but again was yanked to the ground as Drake nudged the heavy chunk of cement down into the well.

The falling weight tightened the rope robbing DC of the slack he needed to escape the trap. He slammed onto the brick pavers that were so intricately placed years ago and slid on his stomach towards the well's side as the block made contact with the water below. The sinking weight pulled tighter and tighter as DC took his panicked last look around through his eyes which were failing due to every blood vessel in them exploding as he choked to death as the dark night faded away. Faded away into nothing. DC's body went limp and again, all was silent. On the outside of the house anyway.

17 FALLING

Knowing they still had two more angels in the house to deal with both Tomek and Drake stepped into the kitchen through the back door the same way DC had run out. They knew their foes had guns but the twins held them in very little regard. From what they had seen they were now hunting boys, not men and certainly not deputies. Drake with his knives in grip stood next to Tomek who had his new bow in hand. He had grown fond of the new Predator three-piece takedown recurve bow Hawkins had given him. The Michigan made bow was much prettier than his self-made bows of days gone by and was deadly accurate.

Entering the door and seeing the body lying in the kitchen floor, split in half from the window slamming down upon his stomach, they grew more curious as to what had happened. Drake reached over to the wall and flicked a switch turning on the kitchen and dining room lights.

"Who the hell do you think did that?" Tomek asked.

"These guys are nothing short of animals, pure ghetto bred heathens. They probably did it to each other. They disgust me. Truthfully, we are doing the world a favor, let's kill them all just so we don't have to deal with them later," Drake said showing his brother he clearly viewed the angels as less than human.

"What about her?" Tomek asked.

"You know why we are here, when we find her we will deal with it our way," Drake answered.

Tomek then reminded his brother "Yea, but Hawkins said,"

"Hawkins said protect her from the angels, we are doing that," Drake then continued "But he sure as shit didn't say what to do with her after that," Drake replied.

"So what is the plan?" Tomek asked.

Drake took a longer pause than before to answer, "I don't know, I just don't okay."

"Yea," Tomek said.

"We tried to kill her, then she tried to kill us. Fair is fair right? Or no, I wish I knew what Uncle would do," Tomek pondered aloud but his thoughts quickly turned back to their current task at hand as they heard the floor boards in the living room area creak warning them that someone was approaching.

Drake slinked into the corner with his back flat against the wall panty's cupboard doors waiting for the unknowing victim to step into the dining room while Tomek covered his back entering the kitchen with an arrow nocked. They waited and waited but heard and saw nothing for almost twenty minutes. Tomek grew restless and entered the dining room signaling to Drake that he was going to head back outside and around the front of the building where he would then enter through the front door. This way they thought whoever was hiding in the living room area trying to wait them out would think they had left while truly being flanked and surrounded.

Exiting out the back door, Tomek let it slam shut to build the illusion that they had left. He then circled the wooded and ivy-covered side of the brick house passing over a small garden area and metal bike racks finding his way to the front porch. Slowly entering the front door, all stealth was now lost as it creaked open as if they were watching one of the campy old scary movies that Hawkins was fond of on late night television.

With the creaking of the door, Gabriel sprang up to his feet and began running full speed from the living room towards the back door of the dining room trap that Drake had set perfectly for him.

"Coming your way!" Tomek yelled letting his brother know to get ready. Tomek drew his bow back but the combination of dark and a running target did not give him the clearance he needed for a shot. Letting the arrow down he chased after Gabriel.

As Gabriel jumped over the hole in the floor his landing area was directly in front of Drake. Drake saw the flash of his body as it entered the doorway and he swung at Gabriel with his knife in a backhand motion fully expecting to make contact with the angel's chest and drive the blade deep into the heart. Only there was no Gabriel there, no chest, and no heart. Drake had missed completely and the off-balance clumsiness of not making contact spun him around the door's edge causing his momentum to fling him down to the ground on his side.

Rolling over, he looked up to see what had happened just as he saw Gabriel blast through the screen door. Getting back up to his feet, he took two bounds and knew exactly why his previous strike had landed nothing but air. Looking down it was clear to see on the smeared linoleum floor that after he jumped the hole, Gabriel had landed in the blood of the dead window boy, started slipping and fell backward avoiding the swinging knife as if he was doing a life and death version of the limbo game.

Drake got up, slipped on the blood himself, and regained his balance before hitting the ground and followed the bloody footsteps of Gabriel out the door and into the wood line. Tomek moving through the living room, watched as his brother was leaving the house. In an effort to join his twin, Tomek took a running start and leaped in the air to bound over the hole that unbeknownst to him, held his sister at the bottom who had stayed silent this entire time just observing what she could of the action happening above her.

Upon reaching the opposite end of the hole, Tomek's foot broke through the weak and dry-rotted historic wooden flooring. The area cut by the angels had deteriorated the entire section of flooring and as he dropped through it, his bow and the nocked arrow were ripped from his grip and tumbled downward into the cellar landing at Henderson's feet. If not for Tomek's outreached grip on one of the floor joists, he would have the same fate as his bow, and his sister.

Tomek hung there, from one arm strung out dangling above Henderson and yet at this point she was unaware of exactly who was above her. Henderson picked up the bow and felt around for the arrow. In a short matter of seconds, she had found the arrow and had it nocked onto the string. Feeling the smoothness of the bow's wood and the manufactured quality of it made her think there was no way it was a weapon that her brothers could have made by hand. Therefore the thought of it being Tomek dangling above her had yet to cross her mind. Until she heard his voice and not only was it his voice, it was what he yelled.

"Drake, help!" Tomek screamed his brother's name in a desperate attempt of his voice reaching his twin's ears outside of the house. "Drake, Cemel Dosce!" Tomek yelled again.

Having reached the wood line following Gabriel's tracks, Drake heard his brother yell for help but ignored it knowing that whatever Tomek was dealing with Drake knew he was capable of handling it on his own. Drake had taken two more steps into the wood line's thicket when he heard the Latin.

"Cemel Dosce," Tomek yelled again. This time Drake stopped in his tracks turned and began sprinting back to the house. Tomek continued to yell, but it was no longer Tomek's voice Drake was hearing, it was Uncle's.

When you boys are in trouble, I mean dead-like trouble you must ask for help from each other but also from yourself. Your inner beast must fight for you as hard as your fellow twin beast does. Call out your beast with Cemel Dosce which in Latin means know thyself. With this call you will summon yourself and your brother to your aide. Use it sparingly and always remember to know thyself.

Drake had never heard Tomek use the call, not when dealing with a bear, not when fighting a deputy, and not even when drowning inside the flooded cabin. But hanging there, ready to fall into the unknown darkness Tomek yelled it again, with all his might.

Henderson's shoulder and arm still injured from her fall throbbed with pain, but she fought through it in pulling the nocked arrow back. Unable to hold it for more than a mere second or two she let it down again in order to get a better shot up through the broken floorboards at her hanging little brother that was like a giant piñata full of hate. She knew from their unexpected showing at the funeral that they had survived, but until this moment she was not totally sure if it was them on that roof top or not. Now there was no doubt. Still as she pulled back and tried to aim at Tomek her mind raced on, wondering, asking if she could actually kill her own blood again for a second time.

"Cemel Dosce!" Tomek yelled as he attempted to swing his free arm up to grab onto the joist. His attempt failed and he remained there waiting to be saved or to fall, whichever came first. The blood inside his veins drained from his grip causing his hand to begin losing both strength and its color. Tomek looked down into the dark and saw nothing. The thought of nothing below him scared him more than if was able to see what he would land on. Be it spikes or water he certainly didn't think that it would be his sister there in the hole.

With the bow pulled back again Henderson looked down the arrow shaft trying to line up the center mass of Tomek's body. With only one arrow this was her only chance. She knew if he fell and landed without being injured she would not be able to take him on in a fight being that her current condition barely let her draw back the bow. Aiming, looking at her brother the string touched her check and found its anchor. She was not an archer by any means, but she remembered the basics from her weekends spent at Camp Linden. The Girl Scouts camp where her original love for the outdoors had bloomed. At this point she convinced herself that shooting Tomek was no different than a Camp Linden hay bale.

Henderson pictured the bull's eye target on her brother's back just as Drake entered the kitchen door two floors above her. Peering through the dimly lit kitchen, all he could see was the black hand of his brother, protruding up from the hole where it held on for life white knuckled. Sprinting towards the hole, Drake's stomach sank as he saw his brother lose what little grip he had left. Diving to his stomach sliding through the blood, Drake reached down finding the strap to Tomek's back quiver.

Grabbing the strap and pulling up instantly stopped Tomek's descent and almost yanked Drake into the hole himself in return. Yet there they stayed, Drake at the top of the hole laying prone out on his chest in the pool of blood holding his swinging brother. Tomek reached up, grabbing Drake's free hand and they held tight to each other as if it was some type of a Russian trapeze act they had performed under a circus tent a thousand times.

Growing up in the woods with Uncle, there was certainly no circus and never a trapeze but death pits were nothing new. They worked in them for most of their teenage lives and often the only way out was to be lifted up. The only thing different from this pit than the rest is they didn't dig it first. Yet getting out of it from this point was fairly easy for them. Drake wedged his feet around the legs of the heavy wood carved kitchen dinner table as Tomek pulled himself up gripping on to and using Drake's body as if it was a ladder. Drake in return grabbed and held onto each piece of Tomek's clothes that he could lifting him up as his twin brother climbed.

The climbing procedure took less than ten seconds and as Tomek neared the top, Henderson let down the bow's string. It was not her injury that kept her from releasing the string and shooting at her brothers, it was her heart.

Getting up to their feet Tomek looked at Drake and simply nodded. Drake knew he was being thanked and the nod was enough for him. Words did not need to be exchanged. While Drake had no words for his brother in return he did have something else to say. Stepping over the hole, Drake looked down into the small area of the cellar that was filled by the overcast light of the dining room and said,

"Hey, mouse, you should have killed us when you had the chance, you dumb bitch."

Henderson knew her hiding spot inside the pitfall trap was now known. Out of anger she quickly drew back the bow again and waited for Drake to lean back over once more exposing any part of his body. This time she would be sending an arrow his way. But neither Drake nor Tomek leaned back over to peer down at her because as they turned around to exit out the back door Father Niko's archangel Michael stood there looking at them. Michael was not going to run like Gabriel, he was there for one reason, to fight. Standing there, bleeding slowly with a piece of his ear missing thanks to Tomek's tendency to keep trophies the angel seemed confident and prepared for battle. As if he truly had God on his side.

Michael motioned the twins to come towards him with just his index finger in a come-hither motion as if he was calling a puppy and said,

"Hello Twins, time to join your Uncle, in Hell."

18 COMBAT

Looking at each other and then back at Michael, the twins were taken aback by the brashness of the archangel. Bowless, Tomek stood there without a weapon. Drake held a knife in each hand and was prepared to fight a hand-to-hand battle. However both boys figured the rifle in Michael's hands would not make this a fair fight. The angels next action was just as curious as his first.

Michael removed the rifle's sling from around his neck and shoulders and dropped it to the ground where the metallic receiver and wooden stock made a thud causing both twins to flinch thinking a round might fly out. He then removed the semiautomatic pistol from his hip. The twins stood there frozen waiting for his next move knowing that if he was going to simply just shoot them he would have done so when their backs were turned earlier. Releasing the magazine detention from the grip the ammo hit the floor. Michael then racked the slide back ejecting the remaining round in the chamber into the air where it cart wheeled onto floor as well. Dropping the useless weapon, he now stood in front of the twins, weaponless.

Reaching back into the corner of the door, Michael picked up the wooden baseball bat that Henderson had kept there for beating the dust out of her rugs on the back patio. Aside from the fact that there were two of them to his one, the fight had become fair.

The three of them circled each other,

"You sure you want to do this?" Tomek asked as if he was warning Michael about exactly who he was dealing with.

Michael just smiled and answered them with scripture recanting David's battle with Goliath, "Thou comest to me with a sword, and with a spear, and with a shield: but I come to thee in the name of the LORD, the God of the armies of Israel, whom thou hast defied."

His answer only confused the brothers more so than before, but no matter their confusion, they knew that keeping their focus and killing the angel was their only option. With the ending of Michael's rant, Tomek grabbed a plate from the countertop and threw it Frisbee style at the head of the angel while in a simultaneous motion Drake hurled a throwing knife at his abdomen. The boys quickly realized this fight might be more difficult than they expected as Michael caught the plate that was meant to be a distraction and used it to deflect the thrown blade just inches before it reached him.

The twins then rushed the angel and launched a barrage of both punches and kicks using all the hand-strike combat techniques that Uncle had trained to his servicemen sent into war over the years. Michael did not strike back, he only used his arms and body along with the bat to block each of their deadly advances. The angel pivoted and spun as both Tomek and Drake came from separate angles trying to penetrate his self-imposed layered of defense. It was as if Michael was faster than what the twins thought to be humanly possible. Somehow he could see every attack coming at him as if in some sort of a trance. None of their strikes found their mark.

Michael was never the biggest angel in Father Niko's arsenal, but he was the baddest. Known to Niko as the silent killer, only his faith in God was stronger than his devotion to Niko. Michael's years of martial arts training had led him to this moment. All the hours of sacrifice and prayer had formulated him into not just an angel but an angel of death. Tomek, out of breath, looked away for just a mere second and felt the blow of the bat against his ribs dropping him to the ground. The angel of death was now on the offensive.

Michael then swung the bat around like it was a weapon he had trained with his entire life and stepped closer to Drake, who like his brother was out of breath but squared up to the angel ready for another round. Michael with the bat draped across the back of his shoulders, held the butt-ended handle with his right hand and pointed his left shoulder towards Drake. With a glancing swing kick to Drake's knee he tumbled to the ground where a quick brush of the bat across his shoulders made contact with Drake's lowered face. With his guard down, the wooden concave bat end found its mark breaking Drake's nose sending a fine mist of blood into the air.

The next blast of the bat was upon the top of the back of Drake's head. The blow dropped him to his stomach unconscious and useless in any rescue attempt for his brother who had once again regained his composure and stood up trying to draw in a full breath to his injured chest. Michael walked towards the remaining twin slowly and methodically.

"I watched what you did to my angel at the well. And now I am going to do the same to you," said Michael.

"Hey, Thou shall not kill, remember?" Tomek said backing away from Michael realizing for the first time since he was locked drowning in the underground cabin that he was afraid.

"Oh yes, I know the commandments. Yet the gospel of Matthew tells us an eye for an eye and well, you know what, I tend to rather like the gospel of Matthew so therefore you shall receive the same fate as you put upon DC," Michael continued talking while slowly walking Tomek back into the corner breakfast nook area.

"That well, shall be, your grave!" Michael methodically yelled as he squarely kicked Tomek in the breastbone sending him tumbling back over the small bench of the nook and crashing through the window's glass panes. If the homerun swing to his chest was not enough, Tomek was now laid out on the brick pavers of the backyard area covered in glass and lacerations. Tomek felt as if his skin wept blood from every inch like a horde of rats trying to escape a sinking ship.

Looking back to the floor where he left Drake sprawled out bleeding from a destroyed nasal cavity, Michael was shocked to see the space empty. Drake's body was missing. Walking back over to the area of the floor where he originally left him, the trail of blood drips from Drake's face was evident on the floor. Michael followed the blood to the back door where it exited outside. Planning all along to toss the both of them down the stone well, this worked perfectly into his overall plan.

Stepping out the back door, Michael looked to his left and was at least grateful to see Tomek still there on the cobblestones. Not knowing the exact location of the missing twin wasn't much of a concern at this point as the blood drips continued around the side of the house revealing to Michael the path of Drake's escape.

"Ouch, that looks painful," Michael said while walking over to Tomek looking at the various cuts caused by the old-styled leaded glass window.

The angel reached down and grabbed Tomek by the collar of his tiger-striped Vietnam-era camouflaged shirt and drug him over towards the well stopping at the side. Tomek provided no resistance until reaching the damp, dew-covered mossy fieldstone side of the well.

Reaching up with both hands, Tomek gripped onto Michael's lowered wrist and twisted his body over rolling up onto his shoulder while lifting both of his legs up and around the angel's upper arm. Tomek then locked his ankles together on top of Michael's shoulder and pulled back down with all his body weight locking his opponent into an arm bar technique. Tomek lurched backward with all his weight and remaining strength, attempting to dislocate the elbow and break every bone in Michael's arm.

While the arm bar had caught him off guard, Michael was trained in defending against it and went to the ground in the same direction as Tomek tugged in an attempt of go with the flow of momentum and not against it. Pushing his arm deeper into the grip of Tomek Michael counteracted the remaining handhold set against him. Combining the weakened grip with lubrication in the form of his own blood, Tomek was unable to apply the grip and pressure needed to successfully break Michael's arm. Feeling his hands slip and twist around the single arm he held, Tomek lost his grip and Michael's arm was free. Tomek rolled to his right and got to his feet before Michael could do the same and as he ran towards Niko's archangel he focused on the bottom of the jaw and raised his leg in a kicking motion with all his force knowing that if it connected, his opponent's jaw would be broken and the tide of the fight would turn his way.

Again to his surprise, the tide did not turn. Michael was still one move ahead of Tomek in this chess game of death. Dropping backward and arching his back, the black combat boot of Tomek glanced off of his cheek causing no more damage than just a tiny scrape. Tomek's momentum carried through due to the missed kick spinning him around to face away from Michael.

Tomek quickly found himself flat on the ground again after Michael buried his fist into the lower back of the twin sending a decimating ripple of pain into Tomek's kidneys. Grasping at his midsection, Tomek rolled over and saw his brother Drake now standing behind Michael and was instantly relieved. Michael noticed the glare of Tomek's eyes change and instinctively looked back to see Drake standing there with a single throwing knife in his hand. Michael stood there, bat in hand, waiting for the next move.

Tomek remained on the ground, in pain watching the seconds tick by as if they were hours. No words were spoken as all three of them, just watched each other. Each of them breathing heavy ready to continue this ultimate battle of life and death. Only the twins had been wounded but the silence confirmed that in some way, the three of them had an unexplainable sense of respect for each other.

The respect would only last until death as Drake whipped his forearm forward holding onto just the tip of the knife blade. He felt it rotate out and away from his hand. Spinning towards its mark the blade buried deep upon impact. Slicing and splintering its way into it's target, the blade stopped upon reaching its bolster.

The three of them again stood there, looking in disbelief at the effectiveness of the simple hand-knapped stone blade. Michael looked down at his chest expecting there to be blood, but there was none. He looked up and smiled at Drake because baseball bats do not bleed. The knife had slammed into the sweet spot of the wood bat and remained lodged there. Drake had missed by inches and with this last failure, he was out of options.

Fighting the angel by hand had proven to be useless and now their only remaining weapon had been rendered useless as well. Drake squared up, wiped the blood away from the open wound still inside his broken nose and prepared for another battling round of hand-to-hand combat, one which he fully expected to lose. Again, acting as the aggressor, Drake took three quick steps in Michael's direction but never actually threw a punch or kick.

The sound was strange to them both, as if the air had been parted by something. It was not unlike an arrow in flight but much faster, the projectile somehow seemed to disrupt the air pressure around them.

There was no zipping or zinging noise like that of a bullet flying by and the hum of an arrow's fletching was not present. Yet that was the first thing both Drake and Tomek saw as the fallen angel lay there on the ground between them, fletching. Fletching, plastic fletching, vanes with a right helical twist to be exact. Two blue in color and one maize. The vanes rested against the spot where Michael's left eye normally would have been before it was shot out. The razor sharp metal three-bladed trocar tipped broad head protruded out the back of the angel's skull. The black graphite shaft of the short arrow puzzled them as this type of equipment was unknown to them.

Looking to the dark ridge of bushes where the short arrow had come from, both Tomek and Drake watched as one of the bushes seemed to come alive and stand up. The shooter in a full ghillie suit stood there looking at them. Their savior's identity was hidden by the suit's mask and face paint. The bush person held a crossbow and the twins now realized the short arrow was not an arrow at all but a crossbow bolt. Having never owned or even shot one the weapon was foreign to them. The only knowledge of the crossbow would be from its primitive use in the medieval history teachings of Uncle.

Reaching up the and pulling back the hood of the suit, it was clear who had saved them. The back porch area while not well lit, did have enough of an open sky to allow the shining harvest moon to illuminate the face of this mystery subject with a talent for a strange form of archery. Standing there smiling with an *I told you so,* kind of look, Old Man Hawkins had yet again made good on the promise he made to his twin brother. Hawkins had just killed Father Niko's archangel Michael in order to once again save and protect the boys.

"Thank you," Drake said in a tired loss for words manner spitting blood out of his mouth that had drained from inside his nasal cavity.

"You are welcome, now get up." Hawkins said motioning to Tomek. "We have some tracking to do."

"Tracking?" Tomek asked.

Hawkins pointed to the ground and said "That's what this blood trail says. How many angels are left?"

"Just one," Tomek answered.

"Which one?" Hawkins asked.

"Not sure, bigger one. I think they called him Gabriel or something like that." Tomek said.

"Gabriel, huh" I figured he would be the first to run. I always hated the little bitch," Hawkins uttered in his disregard for the thug.

"Yeah but, he is not bleeding, he must of picked up some blood on his shoes from inside. Once that is gone, how do we track him down in the dark with just his spoor?" Drake asked.

"Spoor?" Tomek asked chuckling and rolling his eyes knowing full well where his brother had picked up the word but still amused at his use of it.

"Yes, it means..." Drake began to say before being interrupted

"His track, I know what spoor is. Uncle made us both read the same African hunting books," Tomek said trying to show up his brother and impress Hawkins at the same time.

"Ah yes, that Uncle of yours always did enjoy the writings of the legendary Peter Capstick Hathaway. Am I correct in assuming this is the spoor author of which you speak?"

"Yes," the twins answered in unison.

"Very well then, follow the spoor and let us go track down an angel," Hawkins said as he pushed his way into the hip tall saw grass.

"We don't have much blood, and the muck will cover his foot prints, how do we track him?" Drake again asked.

Hawkins just smirked and said, "We don't, Sypris does."

19 ROPE

For the first time in what seemed to be a lifetime in the pit, the house was quiet. There was no stomping around, no yelling and all the fighting had made its way out to the back yard. Although the violence had moved outside, Annette Henderson still lay trapped at the bottom of her coal cellar a mere twelve feet from the freedom of her basement floor.

Unsure on who had won the fight that had raged out above her, she was sure no matter who the victor was she would soon be on their to do list of kills. Not willing to become a victim, she again flicked the lighter's brass top open and sparked a flame. Again taking in what she had around her, it was nothing more than a random mess of broken beams, the bow, one arrow, and the dead body of Brooks. Henderson felt more despair than any moment before. The pain in her arm had subsided but for some reason she wished it had not. At least the constant pain gave her something to focus on.

Knowing the cellar's heavy wooden doors were held tight and locked on the exterior thanks to their cast iron hinges and locks, her only option was to go up. She then started thinking about different scenarios she was put through during her time in the academy.

Instantly she thought back to a first aid class where the instructor had taught the tourniquet technique for stopping a heavy blood spurting situation such as the loss of a limb. The instructor had sliced shoe laces and denim jeans in order to concoct a make shift apparatus that when tied together and spun around a limb would cut off the victim's circulation to the wound therefore preventing blood loss. Henderson intended to use this same lesson on resourcefulness only she had no need for stopping blood loss. It was not a tourniquet she would be making after all, it was a rope.

Henderson bent down and had her laces removed from her boots within minutes. Many of the guys in her department had laughed about Henderson's use of 550 paracord as boot laces. She had read about it in a survival magazine, but the truth be told, the real reason she used the strong synthetic rope like cord for her boots was a little bit of laziness. The 550 would not fray or come unraveled and that meant she got longer life out of it than normal laces. In return, this meant easier long-term care.

The speed at which she moved and felt her way around in the dark had surprised even her. Placing both of her boot laces in a pile at the center of the room in order not to lose them in the dark she went over to the corpse of Brooks' and harvested his laces as well. Knowing Brook's laces were nowhere near the strength of her own she cut them into three pieces of close to equal length utilizing the sharp arrow head as a knife and then began braiding them as if they were the pony tail of a daughter she may never have.

Interfusing them with the best square knot she could remember, the situation made her giggle. Perhaps it was her way of breaking the tension in the pit or an attempt to clear her mind, but in tying the knots a wealth of fond memories flooded out from her past.

"Right over left, left over right, makes the knot neat, tidy and tight," Henderson said aloud to herself reciting the chant from her days spent in a green vest that was of course adorned with every merit and duty badge possible. Being a Gold Award winning girl scout meant knots were just one of the many things that a led her into a life time of public service. Her shared training and history in the scouting world as well as a deputy had gotten her about seven-feet of rope.

Continuing to look around the room, she knew she needed more but was out of options. Moving the lighter back and forth searching for answers in the darkness that she knew didn't exist, a glint of silver caught her eye. Feeling silly that she had not noticed it before. Brooks' belt was made of leather and his thirty-six-inch waist band would give her another three feet of rope. Removing the belt was quick work and the metal latch made attaching her previous section easy. No square knot was required.

Now with almost ten feet of handmade improvised rope her plan was to attach a heavy plank of wood to one end and throw the plank up onto her basement floor. Pulling it towards her, Henderson thought maybe just maybe it would catch on something, get hung up or at least span a corner of the opening and provide enough support for her to climb out. To her, it was as good a plan as any, but at this point she knew that after tying the rope to a plank, she was still about three feet short of what she would need to at least attempt her escape by climbing out of the cellar. Looking around the room there was nothing, nothing that came to mind other than the bow string. Removing the bow string would leave her defenseless and she figured it would not hold much weight when pulled straight down. Still though, she saw no other choice and soon the string was wrapped around a sizeable plank of the cut floor joist. Picking up the plank and balancing it on her outstretched cupped hands, she wobbled back and forth under the weight of the wood. As if she was competing in a caber toss event at the Pine Run Highland Games, Henderson tossed the wood up into the air and out of the pit.

Getting the wood air borne was the entire plan, getting out of the way of its crashing back down towards her was not. The plank failed to land on the basement floor and stay in place. Luckily, It did however miss her upon its return to the cellar floor as she dived out of the way watching the plank land within inches of her left knee. Not only was her first attempt a failure, but it was clear that once in the air she could see her rope was still in dire need of length.

Straightening out the tangled mess in which the rope had become during the fall she once again lit the lighter in order to see better exactly what she was dealing with. Again looking at the dead young man in the corner she noticed how a nail head that protruded from the beam she tossed had ripped into the denim of his pants. The room was well lit at that point by both the lighter in her hand and the glowing light bulb figuratively burning above her head.

Grabbing the arrow head she began cutting long strips of denim from the angel's pants. The strips when tied together and then woven into the rest of her rope which provided the length that was so very badly needed. With her new multi-piece rope in hand Sheriff Henderson again held the plank vertical and began pushing off with all the strength in her legs as she lifted her hands sending the board up and out of the hole. This time she stood back adding more of an angled trajectory which guaranteed the plank to land on the basement floor.

Successful in her toss, she began to slowly pull the denim section of the rope back towards her dragging the board across the floor boards above. Slowly, inch-by-inch the board slipped back towards the opening until it reached the side edge of the hole. Henderson knew the board was long enough to span the hole, and she only needed it do so to allow her to climb out. Letting out some slack in the rope she backed up against the small incline that lead up towards the door. Once reaching the door, she placed her back against it.

Drawing in a deep breath, she yanked backwards with enough force sliding the plank across the opening with enough momentum to fight the gravity as it crossed the opening. Due to the darkness, Henderson could not see the plank's current position, but she knew it hadn't fallen and that was a great thing. Pushing her back up against the door, she felt pain surge into the top of her shoulder accompanied by a deafening sound that shot into her ears simultaneously.

Henderson dropped to the ground raising her hand up to her ear. The wetness of her blood ran warm upon her hands and she was still clueless as to what had caused it. Sliding her hand down from her ear to the rounded edge of her shoulder bone, she found her shirt practically ripped open and a large chunk of serrated skin and meat had been sliced off. Holding the lighter up to the door she knew what had caused her injury, the same blade that was responsible for cutting open the floor hole, now held her captive. The metal blade of the reciprocating saw had protruded its way through the door she leaned against and provided her with her newest injury.

The noise returned as Annette watched the blood-covered white and red serrated blade of the saw viciously dash in and out of the wooden door. She knew the first attempted toss was loud and figured she had alerted someone to her presence in the cellar. The sheriff knew her options were limited. Either there was an angel coming in to kill her, or perhaps to check on their fallen angel and then kill her. Or worse yet, the day of reckoning was here and her brothers had finally come for their revenge. None of the prospects seemed more attractive than the other and Henderson quickly made her way to the rope.

Reaching up as high on the bottom denim section as she could Henderson wrapped the bottom part of the line around her leg and across the top of her foot where she clamped down upon it with her opposite foot. Climbing out on this skinny and weak of a strand with just her upper body strength would be all but impossible now. Even without the injury to her elbow from the original fall and her now sliced open shoulder blade, the climb would have been iffy. Using her legs and holding tight was her only option. Pointing the lighter towards the door she checked once more as the blade continued making a large square cut. Closing the lid, the room fell back to pitch black and Henderson for the first time placed her entire body weight on the rope and board. It held, to her surprise without as much of a hint of stretch or breaking. The solidness of her escape plan built confidence in her mind and she again pushed up with her feet climbing the rope as if it was middle school gym class all over again. Only at the top of the rope there was no bell to ring, there was freedom, or at least the illusion of it.

Once again Henderson worked her way up and quickly found herself near the top. This was the part of the plan she had yet to figure out in her haste to start climbing. Transitioning off of the rope and onto the board would be the most difficult part. Hearing the square pieces of door fall and hit the ground from its having been cut open, she knew the moment was now. Now or never and with that she let her grip go with both arms and forced them up to the board where they found a light grasp. With her legs still wrapped up in the rope she tried to pull herself up unsuccessfully. Looking back down there was emptiness in the pit other than a bright light and yelling voice.

The tunneling beam of light was so bright that it overwhelmed her and it was as if she was staring into the face of an oncoming locomotive engine. Knowing she hung there on the edge of life and death, the idea of letting go to fall into a quick death seemed peculiar. Strange or not, the grip loosened from her weakened and tired fingers and Henderson felt herself falling. Falling towards the bright white light. This time she would land flat on her back, this time she would not survive. Who had cut through the exterior door and into her shoulder to kill her no longer mattered. She had been saved before they could complete their devilish task.

The impact was not as hard as she had expected it to be. The sheriff chalked that up to the fact that perhaps death did not hurt. Opening her eyes she felt as if she was floating. As if God himself had her in His glorious arms and was ushering her through the pearly gates of St. Peter. God knew her name and she heard Him call for her multiple times. She gladly opened her eyes to look up at Him and just as she had believed she was dead she now knew that was not so, not yet anyway.

Shaking off the confusion and allowing her eyes to focus it was evident that she was not floating at all. She was now being carried. Much like a small child who had gone down for a midday nap, Henderson was in the arms of an angel. It was not the voice of God calling her name and there was no pearly gates. Sheriff Annette Henderson was very much alive thanks to the ability of her unsuspected hero that caught her just as she fell towards the illuminating whiteness of his flashlight.

She certainly never expected of all people to be in his arms. However she was grateful for the surprising rescue. Looking up at his face, she knew that the already long night had just gotten more interesting. Trooper Common would now be joining the investigation.

20 SPOOR

Twenty-five yards into the thick switch and sawgrass both Tomek and Drake were impressed with the speed and skill Sypris showed in following the track that Gabriel had inadvertently left behind in his hasty attempt at fleeing from Henderson house. The small dog mixed up her speeds with both running and trotting keeping her nose low to the ground. Her long floppy ears wafted scent into her wet nose as she had no doubt about what her final goal was.

"I cannot believe she is this good, we have not seen blood in almost three-hundred yards." Drake said.

"Yeah but she may be leading us in the wrong damned direction so we shouldn't be giving her a gold medal just yet. After all like you said, there is no more blood," Tomek replied.

"It is not the blood she is after," Hawkins said.

"What?" Drake asked.

Hawkins smiled and continued on, "Just like when I use her to track down wounded deer, it is not just the blood. It is the scent of the animal she singles out. Gabriel is now that animal and we will find him, sooner than later, so be ready."

"We have circled back towards the house, how come?" Tomek asked.

"Because, that is what Gabriel did," Hawkins answered with confidence.

Working their way out of the mosquito filled fields that surrounded the property, the three of them and Sypris alike were happy to be back onto a main trail that led down to one of the creek areas that fed into the river. Upon reaching the creek, Sypris stopped for a drink.

"Ha, she was just thirsty," Tomek said still skeptical of the Dachshund's abilities.

"Negative," Hawkins replied. "She is tasting the water and checking it for scent. She needs to know if he went up or downstream. The little ass hat must know we are tracking him and started moving through the water. That shit only works in the movies, I bet he did not count on a dog who can track over water."

"For real?" Drake asked not doubting just in a pleasantly surprised manor.

Hawkins did not have to answer Drakes inquiry, Sypris did so for him herself as she took back off following the downstream flow of the creek that would lead back by the far west side of the property and eventually out to the main road.

Following another seventy five yards, Sypris left the creek bed and moved back onto land and which time her nose left the ground and pointed straight up into the air. Following with her nose air bound, she stopped at the gate of the small Henderson family burial plot.

The cemetery had not been used in many years and most of the headstones had withered due to a combination of old age and a severe lack of maintenance. Still a few of the larger decretive burial dressings had survived the years of Mother Nature's lament. Sheriff Henderson had cleaned up the area but had left much of it to be finished on a later date. The final resting place of her great-grandparents was clearly marked by a still standing nine-foot limestone crucifix. The name Henderson had been carved into its horizontal stone beam. The graves of countless others, both family and employee were strewn about inside the iron-gated area.

Hawkins motioned the twins to come up to his side silently.

"He is close, she has found him. Her nose in the air means she is smelling his body, not his track. Be ready," Hawkins said with whisper.

Looking over Hawkins' shoulder Tomek noticed something "Well I'll be damned, no need to keep looking."

Looking across the cemetery both Drake and Hawkins saw exactly what Tomek did. They could not see Gabriel in the moonlight but the chill in air showed them his exhaled breath rising like a chimney from behind one of the larger typically shaped headstones.

"He must be right up against it, nice eye," Drake said complimenting his brother.

Both twins reached down and were scratching Sypris for a job well done which was met with her rolling over to enjoy a belly rub as well.

"Well, that makes it simple, nice job Sypris, let's go kill him," Tomek said.

"Wait, you boys and I have done in the rest of them. With Gabriel being the only angel left, we need him to talk," Hawkins said.

"Talk?" Tomek questioned. "Nope, no talking needed, he dropped his gun after we peppered his ass with the grenade, time to finish this."

"Yes, talk, you boys do not seem to understand that you are part of something bigger than you know. Pine Run has a darkness that has spread upon it and the darkness comes from the building that burns the brightest. Lucky Trail is more than you or anyone else knows and this is our chance. Our chance to end it all but we need information and that wannabe thug hiding behind a gravestone over there is going to give it to me, to *us* that is," Hawkins said.

"And, what if he won't talk?" Drake asked.

"We make him.," Hawkins simply explained.

"Well, that sounds, fun," Tomek said shrugging his shoulders.

All three of them entered the cemetery grounds moving silently. Hawkins worked a line directly behind the gravestone while Tomek and Drake flanked out to either side, moving in unison as if they had turned into a pride of lions embarking on a kill. Gabriel sat there, looking to his left and right but never behind him. His heavy breathing was evidence that at this point he was still very scared. The cool, hip hop thuggish demon persona he had showed so many times inside Hawkins's store had now all but vanished. This was not an angel they were dealing with anymore. Not in the sense of Michael anyway.

Hawkins quickly closed the distance and stood directly behind the stone. Standing above Gabriel, he knelt down and whispered from the back of the headstone in the ghostliest voice he could think of,

"Get off my grave boy."

Gabriel shot up to his feet looking behind him and saw nothing, nothing but darkness and an ominous fog coming up off of the creek that would soon engulf the burial grounds. Running towards the gated entrance, Tomek stepped out and stood face to face with the angel. Still, at this point, Gabriel thought he was dealing with more than just another boy. To Gabriel, Tomek was a ghost, a spirit perhaps sent from the underworld. Gabriel closed his eyes and imagined the worst. A dark, cloudy, and omniscient soulless creature with red glowing eyes that burned with the fired of Hell. The angel never imagined that he had more to be afraid of in reality than his imagination could ever conjure.

Spinning around, Gabriel ran back toward his original spot. Looking behind him, he glanced to see Tomek not chasing him. As his focus came back to the ground in front of him, Gabriel's heart all but exploded from the shock of seeing the same ghost in front of him again. Only this time on the other side of the cemetery. Drake had stepped out and after looking behind himself, Gabriel dropped to his knees and started to cry aloud. Rocking back and forth screaming as if he was just a small child.

Tomek and Drake had simply pulled the age old twins gag and it worked to perfection. Gabriel had no clue there was two of them and they were nothing more than flesh and bone. To the angel they were a single demon who had come for him to atone for his past behaviors.

As he continued to rock back and forth, Hawkins reached down and around the angel's throat locking him into a choke hold until eventually all the rocking, chanting, squirming, and kicking subsided. Niko's angels had fallen and now one of them was nothing more than a prisoner

Hawkins opened up his backpack and tossed Tomek a thirty-foot piece of braided rope,

"String him up," Hawkins said pointing over to the large stone cross grave marker.

"Hang him on the cross?" Tomek said which got him nothing more than a nod from Hawkins.

"I like your style Old Man," Tomek said as he grabbed Gabriel's legs and helped Drake carry and place the angel at base of the monument.

Wrapping the rope around the chest of Gabriel and then under the armpits, Tomek began draping it over the top and pulled as both Drake and Hawkins lifted. The effects of the prior choke hold had all but wore off and Gabriel came to just as they had finished wrapping the excess line around his arms and ankles. In the short amount of time they had, the twins were impressed with their crucifix lashing skills and felt guaranteed there was no way Gabriel would be getting down on his own accord.

"What the fuck?" Gabriel exclaimed wiggling back and forth in a struggle trying to loosen the ropes that secured him to the cross. Hawkins walked up to the front of the cross and looked up at Gabriel.

"Now, tell me Gabriel, is that your real name?" Hawkins asked.

"Man, fuck you, old man. Fuck you and these little freaks that do your dirty work," Gabriel said as he spit a large amount of phlegm to the ground missing Hawkins but landing near his feet.

Hawkins remained calm and reached down into his bag grabbing a small flexible piece of thin wire with wooden handles on each side. The twins stood there silent, watching, not knowing what Hawkins had in store for the angel.

"Gabriel, I am going to be one-hundred-percent honest with you. I am going to torture you, unless you provide me with the information which I desire. Furthermore, if you spit at me or the boys again, I will take your tongue off and hold you head back so you drown on your own blood. Now do we have an understanding?" Hawkins demeanor showed it was clearly not a bluff, but Gabriel remained indignant.

"Fuck, you, Old, Man," Gabriel said slowly and elaborately as if he was giving directions to a tourist who did not speak English.

"Wrong answer," Hawkins replied.

Old Man Hawkins set the wire at Gabriel's feet and began unlacing and removing the angel's right boot. Gabriel kicked and yelled but his struggle was in vain as he was not accomplishing anything but slowing down the inevitable. Hawkins then retrieved the wood-handled wire. Making two loops of wire he held the shape and wrapped it around Gabriel's middle toe. Nudging it up against the end of the foot the loose wire hung there staying in place thanks to the wooden dowels.

Hawkins's then methodically looked up from his kneeled position and asked "Gabriel, huh, how fitting your name is at this very moment. You see we both know that Gabriel was the voice of God. Now this is your chance to be the voice of Niko. This is your big moment, Gabriel, why did you come after Sheriff Henderson tonight?"

Gabriel rolled his eyes and said, "To play board games, we figured the bitch was lonely so..."

The angel was unable to finish his sentence as midway through it Hawkins' grip on the wooden wire ends tightened as he jerked them in opposite directions. The wire loop tightened, shrank and dug into both the flesh and bone of the middle toe. Hawkins continued to apply the pressure as Gabriel screamed in agony. Tightening his grip Hawkins thrust his arms apart once more and watched as the wires completed their pass through removing the toe from the foot with such force that it shot into the air and sailed over Hawkins' shoulder. With blood splatter across his chest and face, Hawkins stood up grabbed Gabriel's cheeks looking him in the eye and said,

"I would appreciate the truth from now on, and when you have no toes or fingers left, I will only have one more option to wrap this wire around."

Gabriel did not speak, either due to shock or pure fear, but the message was clear.

"He means your dick by the way," Tomek said laughing along with Drake. His comment was only met with a glare from Hawkins that all but told Tomek that his brand of humor was not appreciated at the moment.

"Now, once again what are you and your little band of demons doing here tonight?" Hawkins asked.

"We are not demons, we are angels," Gabriel said defiantly.

"Wrong answer," Hawkins said as he began to wrap the wires around the right thumb of Gabriel. Pulling the wire tight it began to cut into the flesh just as it had on the previous toe.

"Wait, wait, wait, wait," Gabriel pleaded.

Hawkins obliged his request, "Yes?"

"Niko sent us to kill her," Gabriel stated as Hawkins loosened his grip on the wires.

"Why?" Tomek asked next.

"She been costing him a lot of money, doing all these traffic stops and shit. What she did to Tower was just bullshit. The bitch shoots him then hangs his ass in a tree? Come on," Gabriel explained.

Of course the twins did not specifically know anyone by the name of Tower, but they looked at each other and grinned full well knowing that it was not their sister that placed the traffic stop thug in the tree.

However they were happy enough to let her take the blame.

"So you were just going to roll up in here, kill a sheriff and then what?" Hawkins asked.

"I don't know, I swear to God. Father Niko and the mayor make all the plans we just do what they say." Gabriel had gone back to pleading.

"So you just blindly follow orders huh?" Drake said rolling his eyes.

"Yes, I am just a soldier. A soldier of God. God speaks to Niko directly and his will be done," Gabriel's mantra had changed again as if some type of spirit and entered him and rejuvenated his will to live.

"Just a soldier huh, my father killed a lot of Germans who were just following orders and you are just as bad as they were in my book," Hawkins said comparing the angel to a Nazi.

"Listen, old man, I don't know what they had planned. All I can tell you is that we were to kill the bitch and head back to Lucky Trail." Gabriel was once again pleading, but Hawkins knew there was more to the story.

"Who was next?" Hawkins asked.

"What do you mean?" Gabriel said.

"Who was next on your list, you rotten flea bag!" Hawkins yelled as he slammed his knife blade deep into the thigh of the angel causing Gabriel to scream and kick in agony. Hawkins kept the blade inside the body applying pressure allowing the blade to slice deeper and deeper into the wound channel.

"You were, you were next, ahhhhhh!" Gabriel screamed but kept yelling through the pain. "With her dead and you gone they could get a town council and sheriff who would be under their control."

"Thanks, but I already knew that," Hawkins said removing the knife from Gabriel's leg and wiping it clean from the blood while picking up his backpack. He motioned over to the twins and said "Let's go."

"Lets go? Lets go?" Tomek asked.

"Are we just going to leave him there, ill finish him off," Drake said.

"You will do no such thing, are you both blind?" Hawkins asked.

The twins both remained silent for this was a side of Hawkins they had yet to see and were unsure on exactly what was happening.

"Blind?" Tome broke the tension asking.

"Look, listen, feel," Hawkins explained. "We have been followed since picking up the track.

"Followed?" Drake replied as Sypris growled.

"Yes, followed. The three wolves which you have not noticed have been on our track as we were on his. First of all, they smell blood and secondly they smell Sypris," Hawkins said as he scooped up the small tracking dog and placed her in his backpack, a place where she was happy to tag along from.

"Bullshit old man," Tomek laughed. "We would know if there was a pack of wolves on our ass."

"Let's go," Hawkins said as he began walking out of the cemetery and back towards Henderson House.

"What about him?" Drake asked.

"Yeah what about *me*?" Gabriel chimed in still bleeding heavily from his open leg wound.

"He is done, I opened the femoral artery. If God is on his side he will bleed out before the beasts find him. If not well then maybe just maybe he didn't pray hard enough," Hawkins said smiling as he was amused with the level of snark he had just verbally dropped on the twins.

The three of them continued down the trail back to the house. Gabriel's cries for help could be heard almost the whole way back to the house. As they passed the back side of the property, all three of them noticed the cries had stopped. Unsure if it was because they were too far away for the noise to travel or if the angel had finally bled out. Either outcome was fine by them but their question was quickly answered and it was not Gabriel's voice that they heard coming from afar.

The howling cry of multiple wolves sent chills down their spines. Both Tomek and Drake looked at Hawkins with a new found respect.

Turning to them, Hawkins just smiled and said,

"Your Uncle knew men, I know dogs."

21 EMPTY

Outside of Henderson House near the stone well, Hawkins, Drake, and Tomek stood there in disbelief looking at the cut open cellar door. Henderson and her savior were nowhere in sight as the twins and Hawkins slowly walked down the cellar steps checking the area.

"You have got to be kidding me," Tomek said as he picked up his unstrung bow and its string still lying there on the floor bundled up with the other pieces of the rope.

"Yeah I know," Drake agreed "She got away, again."

"I was actually talking about my bow string but yeah that too," Tomek said agreeing with his brother.

"This wood was cut from the outside," Hawkins added.

"By what?" Tomek asked.

"A reciprocating saw, much like the one that I sold to the angels earlier today," Hawkins answered.

"So she didn't escape, she was saved," Drake said.

"Yes," Hawkins agreed.

"By who?" Tomek asked.

"Either by someone who wants her alive or someone who wants to make sure she is dead," Hawkins said as he turned back around walking up the stairs that exited the cellar.

The twins looked as each other, shrugged their shoulders and followed their new mentor up and out of the bowels of Henderson House. Hawkins had grown silent as they walked back to his old beat up pickup truck. The store's success allowed him to buy a new one, but he enjoyed the character of the older Chevy Silverado that adorned the name and logo of The Hawk's Nest General Store upon its doors and bed sidewalls.

The boys each felt indifferent in regards to the thought of their sister being either saved or dead. On one hand her being dead would greatly simplify their lives. Both of them were clearheaded enough about the situation to see that as an overall plus. No longer having to worry about killing her, themselves anyway or even the possibility of her coming after them again was definitely a good thing.

However...

Some part of both of them longed for a reunion. A peaceful one at that. They had talked about it only a few times, but during those chats, the realization came about that if, and it was a big if, but if they all could live together in peace, that would be an acceptable solution. After all, Annette was the only family they had. Hawkins was good to them, but the sheriff was bound to them by blood. And with her new found disappearance, they found themselves torn between the two possible futures.

"Now what?" Tomek asked looking back and forth between Drake and Hawkins.

Drake, had built himself up for this ultimate meeting between him and Annette was at a loss for words and just shrugged his shoulders.

Hawkins then spoke up, "Let's assume that he was telling the truth back there on the cross. That means we need to pay Mr. Mayor a little visit."

"What makes you think he wasn't lying?" Tomek asked.

"People tend to tell the truth when they have a knife in their leg," Hawkins responded.

"Why the mayor? Shouldn't we be going after the priest who sent the angels to kill her?" Drake asked offering insight to his current feelings in regards to his sister.

"Negative, we go for the mayor," Hawkins answered confidently.

"Why not take out the leader, you know, cut the head off of the snake?" Tomek joined his brother in the questioning of the old man.

"Not my circus, not my monkeys," Hawkins responded as he hopped into the front cab of his truck waiting for the boys to follow suit. And they did as they were both quite familiar with the old Polish proverb that Hawkins had just laid upon them. It was something Uncle would often say when it came to things that did not directly involve their survival.

"Not my circus, not my monkeys," Hawkins again retorted as the old truck bumped down the dirt road heading back towards town. They both smiled upon hearing it again. There was something comforting in these moments. While it certainly had nothing to do with a circus it was the reminiscing of Uncle that held their hearts together. Sometimes the moments seemed so real, as if there was no Hawkins and it really was Uncle sitting there next to them in that truck.

Cruising down the dirt backroads headed into town the three of them sat silently. There was no grand plotting scheme or tactical plans being made. The twins just watched the pine trees pass one by one through the headlights as they neared the township limits. Coming into town, Hawkins seemed to be driving on auto pilot and did not hear Drake screaming as he tried to pull Hawkins out of his day dream,

"Watch out for that pot hole!" Drake had yelled three times warning Old Man Hawkins of the table-sized crater in the Michigan road that was typical for this time of the year.

Not hearing the warning meant the truck slammed into the hole at full speed jolting the vehicle into the air sending the unbuckled boys into the roof of the cab. Hawkins stopped the truck, looked over at the boys in a state of confusion and asked,

"What about a taco?"

"Pot hole, I said pot hole, Old Man," Drake explained as they all had a good laugh at the misunderstanding. A laugh that they had not had in quite a while. A laugh that instantly bonded them as they prepared to enter more darkness. The darkness of killing.

As they continued into town, the glow from the fire illuminated the dark skyline.

"What the hell?" Tomek said as he looked down the street and clearly saw a building fully engulfed in flames amongst the flashing lights of the fire departments volunteer trucks. The building cracked and popped and they could feel the heat escaping the raging inferno as the crews helplessly sprayed water upon it.

"Leave the truck here, let's take the woods to Landings Way and then cross the bridge. If we follow the old wood path all those hippies use to jog on until the end we will reach the peninsula. The mayor lives at the end of it, last house." Hawkins said.

Not wanting to get out, Drake hesitated and asked "Is that?"

"Yeah it is, they burnt down my store. Our home, its gone. But as of now they think I am dead and if we keep it that way we have the element of surprise," Hawkins said knowing there was no saving the house or the store at this point. The only keepsake he would have wanted was the picture framed in elk antler of him and Uncle together. The picture he never talked about, was the one that meant the most to him.

Hawkins also knew that with a fire that big in the downtown area the mayor would of course be on scene. And if that fire was truly an arson meant to kill him and the twins, waiting for the mayor in his own home just seemed to be the perfect retaliation.

22 POKER

Hours had passed and it seemed as if the sun would soon be cresting the eastern ridge of the pine thicket over Pine Run welcoming a new day. While Tomek and his twin brother Drake sat, patiently waiting along the wood line to the rear of the house, Hawkins waited on the mayor's front porch. Hawkins had decided to hide, or jump out, or even break into the mayor's home for an ambush. Just as much as he wanted to watch the mayor take his last breath he needed to know what the mayor knew. While a knife to the leg may have worked on an angel hanging from a cross, as a politician the mayor would not be so easy to withdraw the truth from.

The headlights crested the slight hill that led up to the end of the peninsula that culminated at the mayoral home. Stepping out of his vehicle, the portly man lumbered up to the white picket fence gate that enclosed his picturesque front yard. All that was missing from this perfect picture of Americana was the wife, two kids and a dog. Walking to the front steps where Hawkins remained sitting motionless the mayor turned the corner around his cedar-style hedges and jumped backwards upon seeing the man he thought to be dead sitting their upon his own property.

"Hawkins, you, you're, alive!" The mayor gasped.

"Surprised?" Hawkins asked.

"Yes, and relieved of course," The mayor's lying had begun two sentences into their conversation.

"The fire department said you didn't make it out, that there was no way anyone could have survived," the mayor explained.

"Lucky me then I guess," Hawkins commented.

"I was devastated when they called me. I just kept telling myself and praying that you would be okay. But when neither you nor Sypris came out, well, we feared the worst," the mayor said.

"Yeah, I went down state for the night. Had to visit my brother's family." Hawkins began sharing in the telling of lies. Even though the twins considered themselves and Uncle family.

"I came back to find my home was gone and well, I need a place to stay," Hawkins said knowing the mayor was a widower with no kids and had plenty of extra space. He figured the easiest way into the house was just flat out asking.

"Uh, here, you want to stay here um," The mayor said showing off the same discomfort that he did the day of the funeral.

"Yeah, if that's not too much to ask. Just for tonight you know. Until we get things sorted out. I have been on the road all day and now this, this tragedy. I just need a place to sleep, a place among those whom I trust." Hawkins thought he may have just laid it on a little too thick, but the mayor invited him in none the less.

Stepping into the mayor's home, Hawkins fought the urge to slice the fat man's throat as soon as the door closed knowing that he needed to wait. The house was well kept for being that of a single guy. A compliment that Hawkins figured was better given to the maid rather than the mayor himself.

"It has been a while, let's go out back on the deck. You have had a hell of a day and I bet you could use a drink," the mayor suggested.

Not wanting to admit to himself that a drink sounded like a fine idea, Hawkins nodded in agreement and followed the mayor as he waddled his way out back. The wooden deck overlooked a quaint backyard with a small storage shed and a neatly stacked pile of cut and spilt cord wood. Another chore that Hawkins was sure the mayor hired out to be done as the mayor had never purchased the tools necessary to complete such a task from him at The Hawk's Nest. There was nothing ornate or special about the house or the yard other than the wood pile. The only thing making the wood pile remarkable was that Tomek and Drake hid behind it. Leering over the edge watching the entire situation unfold from less that fifteen yards away.

Stepping out of the house's sliding glass door and on to the deck, Hawkins could smell the remnants of smoke in the air. What used to be his store, home, and life's work now lay as a pile of charcoal rubble smoldering into the early morning air. And here he sat, on the deck of the man he was sure sparked the flame.

"Kind of feels like old times huh?" The mayor said as the two of them sat down at the octagon-shaped poker table where they had shared many a night playing cards in years gone by.

"Yeah, old times," Hawkins said rolling his eyes.

"Why did you resurface this table in blue with this God awful cat logo?" Hawkins asked forcing himself into a casual conversation while holding back his rage. The mayor did not answer, he just held out his right hand proudly displaying his college class ring from a state school in Pennsylvania. The gold base held a bright blue gem about the size of quarter. It was very noticeable and the mayor showed it off as much as possible often working it into most conversations.

"Matches my alma mater of course, go Nittany Lions!" The mayor said enthusiastically.

"Go lions," Hawkins said with a sigh while rolling his eyes again. "How about that drink?" Hawkins reminded the mayor thinking he needed it now more than ever.

"Oh yes, Scotch okay?" The mayor asked.

"Scotch is always okay," Hawkins grumbled.

The mayor then walked across the decking to an outdoor bar he had set up. The bar was quite nice and Hawkins often felt somewhat jealous of its design. The mayor placed ice into two glass rocker-style cups and then reached over the top of the shelf for the bottle of Scotch. The twins watched closely waiting for their signal. While Hawkins paid them no attention, he knew exactly where they were. Not that he had seen or heard them, he just knew where Uncle would have been and figured the twins would do the same and he was exactly right.

The mayor then looked over his shoulder to see Hawkins staring off into the distance, enjoying what was left of the night stars as they faded into the sunlight. Seeing that he was not being closely watched the mayor flipped his class ring around on his finger. The twins then watched as the blue gem slid open on a tiny set of hinges swinging down and out of the way. The gems hollow cavity was nothing more than a small storage area for some type of powder that they observed fall into one of the glasses. With his nonchalant surgical like movements they could tell this was not the mayor's first go around with poisoning someone. Perhaps the mayor's dead wife's demise was met as she enjoyed one of his corpse cocktails. The mayor then stirred up both the drinks and set the one containing the powder in front of Hawkins as he returned to the table sliding the gem back into its false resting place.

"Come sit down, you have a lot on your mind enjoy the Scotch, its single malt and a great year." The mayor urged Hawkins to join him at the poker table. Hawkins took up the mayor on his offer and joined him at the table. Reaching over to his left Hawkins grabbed a deck of cards and stared shuffling. The mayor watched as his guest started dealing out five to each of them.

"What's the game?" He asked Hawkins.

"Cowboy Poker of course," the old man replied.

"I am a little rusty, what is that one again exactly?" The mayor again asked pushing his glasses back up on his nose.

"Five card draw," Hawkins answered annoyed that the mayor could not remember even the most simplistic of games.

"Cheers," The mayor said lifting his cup into the air in an attempt to get Hawkins drinking the poisoned elixir that awaited him.

Hawkins in response raised his glass clinking it against the mayor's as he then brought it to his mouth to take the customary sip. In doing so they both were startled by the blowing caution call of a whitetail doe.

"Shhhhwoooooooooo Shhhhhhhwwwwwooo!"

The mayor jumped in his seat almost tipping it over in an attempt to get up and run inside. Hawkins laughed setting his drink down.

"Jesus Christ you live out here and have never heard a deer snort before?" Hawkins asked.

"That's what that was?" The mayor said still shaken up as he started drinking his Scotch by the gulp full.

"Yes sir, something must of spooked her that's all. Probably the smoke from downtown," Hawkins replied knowing that while it did sound somewhat similar to a deer snort it was far too human to have been one. He knew the boys were sending him a warning. He just was unsure in regards to what it was about.

Both men picked up their cards and looked at their hands switching the cards around to organize their hands.

"Five card draw, cowboy poker, how many you want?" Hawkins asked.

"Just one," replied the mayor discarding and taking one off the top of the deck.

Looking at his hand full of nothing Hawkins took three cards for himself. All of which did not help in anyway.

"I am glad we aren't playing for cash right now cause I don't got shit," Hawkins said laying down his hand on the blue felt top.

"Two pair," replied the mayor boastfully as he laid down the eight and ace of spades paired with the eight and ace of clubs. Happy with his meaningless victory he raised his glass and then finished his drink hoping to encourage Hawkins to do the same.

"Price of poker just went up," Hawkins said smiling.

"I didn't think we were gambling, so what do you mean?" The mayor asked.

"Well you got aces and eights, now that is an interesting hand," Hawkins quirked.

"Yeah, how so?" The mayor asked.

"Well, that is called the dead man's hand cause legend has it that, is what Wild Bill Hitckok had when he was shot in the back," Hawkins explained. The mayor then laughed and looked nervously behind him. Thankful that he saw no one there he said,

"Well, looks like I am safe tonight."

"That depends," Hawkins said.

"Oh yeah, I'm confused, on what?" The mayor asked.

Hawkins did not answer he just sat there, relaxed as if he was holding an unbeatable hand in the biggest poker game of his life. The silence is what drove the mayor into a panicked state of nervousness.

"What?" The mayor again asked getting no answer but a smiling Hawkins.

"Did you enjoy your drink?" Hawkins asked.

"Yes, why?"

"Did you notice I haven't touched mine? Hawkins said smirking with an eyebrow raised.

"Yes, it's a good Scotch and I am a little insulted you haven't even tried it," The mayor said yet again pressuring the old man to consume the poison.

"You must really be more observant, Mr. Mayor," Hawkins said getting up from his chair and walking towards his soon-to-be next victim.

"I am not sure I get what you mean?" The mayor said as he remained puzzled.

"I know your little ring trick you fat son-of-a-bitch, I've known it for years. Just never needed to worry about it till tonight. Nice try though, the fire didn't work so you thought you would just poison me, huh?" Hawkins stood in front of the seated mayor who looked up at him in horror.

"Poisoned? God no, it was an antidepressant crushed up. It takes the edge off of a long day, it is how I survive doing this fucking job. I was just trying to make you feel a little better. I was trying to be a good friend," the mayor pleaded.

"Oh okay then, that makes sense. Silly me," Hawkins said taking a step back. Picking up his glass, he once again held it to his mouth and just as the single malt began to flow into his mouth the glass exploded into pieces. Looking down he saw his hand bleeding from the broken glass. He glanced to his right and saw an arrow stuck into the back of the house. Tomek had shot the glass right out of his hand in what he thought was a lifesaving gesture.

Running up from their hiding place behind the wood piles, the twins climbed onto the deck joining the two of them. The mayor's face again looked of both horror and confusion.

"Mowgli, you are real. You are alive? There are two Mowglis?" The mayor knew about the existence of Tomek from the picture shown to him by his former sheriff on the washed up satellite phone but had no clue about the existence of Drake.

"Well, I guess the boys missed the same details of our little poker game that you did there, Mr. Mayor," Hawkins said showing his annoyance by holding up and gesturing with his bloody hand.

"What's that?" asked the now trembling mayor.

"You see that was not a deer snort, that was them," Hawkins began explaining but was interrupted by Tomek,

"Yeah, you are welcome for that and for my shot. I just saved your ass twice Old Man. How about a little appreciation?"

Hawkins looked down at his bleeding hand and seemed less than appreciative. Hawkins continued on enjoying the panicked look on the mayor's face. "Antidepressants huh? Then I guess you have nothing to worry about." Yet the mayor certainly did have something to worry about thanks to his chugging of the Scotch.

"What do you mean I have nothing to worry about?" The mayor asked getting the conversation back on track.

"Well, while you were jumping up and down shitting yourself over a little noise from the woods I switched our glasses," Hawkins claimed.

"You did what?" The mayor asked again, but he knew the answer to his question.

"Like you said, it was just a little antidepressant so you got nothing to worry about right?" Hawkins said as he looked at the twins with a smirk letting them know although they hadn't seen him switch the glasses himself, he was in fact telling the truth.

The mayor dropped to all fours and began coughing, slamming his own fingers deep into the back of his throat in an attempt to make himself vomit up the poison he meant to give Hawkins. The gagging and hurling sound alone was enough to make the others question the integrity of their own stomachs. Yet they stood there watching the large man deposit an enormous amount of what must have been dinner onto the wood planks of the home's deck.

"I know you killed your wife, I know you burnt my home and I know you are going to start telling me why," Hawkins said as he pulled the mayor up to his knees punching him in the ribcage just up and under the arm pit. The blow dropped the politician back to the ground where he now laid chest down in his own vomit.

"You, you need to talk to Niko and that bitch sheriff. I didn't do any of those things. It was all them." The mayor began trying to explain himself.

"I was just out at the sheriff's house, she was in quite the predicament thanks to Niko. So stop with the dime store lies. The more you lie, the shorter your life is going to get," Hawkins threatened the vomit-soaked man who was now openly crying and sat there totally defeated.

"That precious sheriff of yours has been working with Niko all along. She had the keys to the fire trucks, that is why your store burnt to the ground. The fire department couldn't even respond cause they were locked out. Now why do you suppose that was? Cause she knew Niko was going to set it ablaze. I had to go down to city hall and give them the emergency set of keys. If it wasn't for me the entire town would have gone up." The mayor's story made sense, but Hawkins knew that a guilty man always has an alibi.

"Why would the sheriff want me eliminated?" Hawkins asked not buying a single ounce of what the mayor was saying.

"She don't give a damn about you, its Niko. With you gone, he can run the council and he can do as he pleases," the mayor continued. "Henderson gave every bit of those fucking drugs she took off of that traffic stop where the two boys ended up dead back to Niko. That Tower kid was a loose cannon and Niko wanted him gone. He told her when and where and all she had to do was make it happen."

"Uh huh, sure," Tomek piped in.

"It's the fucking truth. Father Niko has some grand plan for saving the souls of those who repent. And somehow both you and Henderson are part of it," the mayor claimed implying Hawkins knew more than he was admitting too.

"Now that is a bunch of beer-battered bullshit your slinging there." Hawkins said.

"She owed Niko for her promotion, and she is helping him get all the narcotics he needs for this so-called master plan of his," The mayor claimed.

Upon hearing that, Hawkins immediately disagreed saying,

"She owed me, not him, nice try. I am the one who nominated her and I am the one who pushed for her to get that job."

"And you think Niko just let that happen?" The mayor asked.

"He didn't have a choice in the matter," Hawkins answered.

"Father Niko always has a choice, his will and only his will be done. And if you think differently, then you're as dumb as he hoped you would be, old man," the mayor said.

The mayor was beginning to make sense but luckily enough before he could be swayed, Tomek walked up and kicked the mayor directly in the face knocking out multiple teeth while smashing his glasses into the bridge of his nose where they snapped and lodged into his right eye socket. The mayor rolled over onto his back, rocking back and forth with his hand over the damaged eye he could feel was popped out of its socket. The man began screaming in terror at the thought of holding his own eye and lowered his hand allowing the disconnected eye to completely roll out of his orbital cavity and onto the deck.

Pulling his bow back, arrow nocked, Tomek was actually looking forward to ending the mayor's misery not to mention the fact that his screaming was getting louder and while the neighbors were not close by they did not need any extra attention brought their way. Looking up with his one good eye at Tomek the defeated mayor began talking while spitting out blood from his mouth,

"Well it looks like you got me in your crosshairs, son."

"I ain't your Goddamned son and bows do not have crosshairs, you fat piece of shit," Tomek replied as the string left his fingers propelling the stone-tipped cedar-shafted arrow directly into the chest of the man where it cleanly sliced through his heart and exited out the back of his torso.

"Hmm, I always figured he would die of a heart attack," Hawkins said smirking as he turned around to face Drake and walk back towards the woods. As he made eye contact with the subject behind him, Hawkins stopped dead in his tracks. Standing there in shock, the old man had to look twice as he believed that his own eyes were deceiving him. It made no sense, how could, why? Hawkins was speechless.

It was not what he thought or even what he saw that rendered him unable to speak. The man who saved the twins, the twin brother of their beloved Uncle, who took them into his home, taught them to adapt and survive inside a functioning society, was speechless thanks to the four-inch steel forged blade of the tactical knife Drake had just thrust deep into his throat.

Hawkins instantly began to choke on his own blood as it ran down both the interior and exterior of his throat and dropped to his knees as the aggressive loss of blood combined with the lack of oxygen quickly did him in. Drake guided his body to the ground keeping him out of the previously spilled vomit and as Hawkins life left his body, his eyes closed and Drake removed the knife. The old man's blood quickly poured out from the wound but within half a minute it stopped as the heart was no longer working at circulating it up and out.

Tomek quickly reached into his quiver, nocked another arrow and drew his bow back aiming at his twin unsure of what exactly had just happened.

Drake looked at his brother, reached around his back without saying a word pulling out the original letter Uncle had given to Hawkins for the boys. The same letter Hawkins had given the twins directly after saving them from the water-filled underground cabin. Drake opened it up slowly showing his brother exactly what it was and reminded him of one of their Uncle's oldest lessons,

"After three the truth you see," Drake said extending his hand out toward Tomek handing over the letter.

Tomek lowered the bowstring and snagged the handwritten parchment from his twin. With Uncle's old saying taken into consideration, Tomek began decoding Uncle's true hidden message. Something he had not thought to originally do. Drake had made it easier by circling the third word of every line.

"After three the truth you see," Drake said again reminding Tomek of Uncle's hidden way of passing along written information that may get intercepted by an enemy. The genius of Uncle's system meant being able to have a true directive hidden inside what seemed to be an innocuous letter.

Instantly Tomek knew that their Uncle's bother, Old Man Hawkins, had to die.

Boys,

This man (I) have given this letter to is,
Someone I (have) entrusted to keep you safe.
Always keep @ clear mind, trust him. He is my brother.
Love your (twin) as I do mine.
He won't (kill) you. He will teach you to thrive.
Learn about (him) and accept his teachings.
Life changes (when) you learn.
I kept (your) lives hidden for protection. I was wrong.
Living in (secret) was wrong. I am sorry.
My death (is) not your fault.
Living life (out) of town is over for you.
Now your (return) to the old ways can never be.
This is (home) now, accept the change.
Now go (to) his home in Pine Run.
Forget our (woods) there is nothing there now.

Be the (snake)
Not the (mouse)
Be strong,
(Uncle)

24 LUCKY TRAIL

The early morning sun had cleared the tall trees that surrounded the entire compound of Lucky Trail by the time Tomek and Drake arrived at the front gates. The hike to reach their current position was a mere thirty-minute trek if they would have gone directly through downtown, but with most of the residents now in the streets surrounding the smoldering remains of The Hawk's Nest the twins were forced to stay out of sight within the wood line. A strategy that sat just fine with them.

For all that Lucky Trail was, the fact that it was not heavily fortified seemed odd to the brothers. It was their understanding that Father Niko housed nothing but troubled kids and they imagined the property to be more reminiscent of the wartime prisons that Uncle had so often told them of. The twins were surprised to see the country club setting that was laid out before them.

Drake carried the crossbow Hawkins had brought to Henderson House along with his normal assortment of throwing and tactical knives. A predator three-piece takedown recurve bow and a quiver full of arrows was all that his twin, who preferred to travel lighter and be less bogged down with equipment, carried.

The long gravel driveway meandered through an open hardwood lot with enough twist and turns that each blind corner had to be crested in stealth mode to protect themselves from walking directly into an ambush. Working their way slowly through the open front gate and past the empty guard houses, they looked inside the small box that sat at the corner of the property. It looked more like a roadside fruit stand than a guard shack but once inside they knew what it was used for.

A small television portrayed a black and white screen shot of multiple camera views. Looking over the feed on the screen it was clear that Lucky Trail was empty. No residents, no guards and certainly no angels. *It made no sense, where was everyone?* They both pondered.

Rummaging through the desk drawers provided nothing useful other than a key to the locker that stood behind them. Opening the lock and looking inside, both Tomek and Drake looked at each other and smiled. Pulling out the contents and lying them down upon the desk Tomek knew what his brother was thinking.

"Here, you take this one," Drake said handing over the forest green polo shirt. The shirts donned the yellow Lucky Trail stitched logo and happened to be same shirt each of the angels they had killed the night before were wearing as they met their demise.

"This uniform is bullshit man, we need to keep our camo on," Tomek said showing his displeasure in dressing like one of Niko's kids.

"Put the dammed thing on and be a wolf," Drake told him.

"A wolf?" Tomek asked.

"In sheep's clothing," Drake replied in reference to the old parable they both had learned from Uncle many years ago.

Tomek understood his brother's plan and began putting on the shirt needing no more encouragement. Drake figured they would remain unseen approaching the main compound areas tactically in silence, but if they were dressed as angels and were seen from a distance they may just be ignored.

Taking one last glance at the closed caption television monitor on the shelf, Tomek caught movement in the corner of the screen. The screen was labeled with a sticker that read Chapel.

"Look here, look at this, there he is," Tomek said grabbing his brother and turning his attention to the monitor. Neither of the boys had actually met or even seen Father Niko before other than from afar on the day of the funeral. However they both knew the man they were looking at. Standing at the pulpit was none other than the Father himself.

Adorned in full ceremonial robes and multicolored sashes of red and purple, the Father seemed to be looking up to the sky. As if he was having a silent conversation with the Lord himself. They could not make out much more due to the graininess of the small screen but knowing his location made their next destination inside the compound an easy choice.

They both continued to watch as Niko swayed back and forth, throwing his arms up above his head, waiving them around only to have them shoot back down towards the earth with the same velocity. There was something captivating about the video feed to the twins. Even with no sound, Father Niko could grab and hold one's attention. It was as if he truly did have a hold on their souls and the boys found themselves watching him and paying no attention to the rest of the world around them. Then the unthinkable happened.

For no known rhyme or reason, Father Niko stopped his apparent preaching and walked to the middle of the red carpeted altar area. There the man stood atop three steps motionless. He then looked up and to the corner of the room, looking directly at the camera mounted where the walls met the roof. Staring with his dark eyes at the lens of the camera he raised his left hand into the air pointing a finger at the camera. Rolling his wrist over, Father Niko the used the same extended finger to make a come hither motion. It was if Father Niko knew he was being watched by the twins and had openly invited them to come and join him in the sanctuary.

Stepping away from the screen Tomek and Drake just looked at each other frozen in shock. It was not fear. The twins did not fear Father Niko. Hawkins had ranted about the priest many times but never portrayed him as anything but a politician like the mayor that wore robes.

"Does he know we are here?" Drake asked.

"There is no way, he must have been telling someone else to come join him. Someone else who was supposed to be in that shack," Tomek said making sense of the situation.

"But, where are they?" Drake responded asking what they both thought.

"Good question," Tomek replied.

"Let's go," Drake suggested.

"Go?" Tomek replied.

"Lets go, we can leave here, leave Pine Run," Drake said.

"Why, are you scared or something?" Tomek asked

"Scared, no. But we have always been taught to survive. Going after Niko does not help us survive. Even if we walk in there and he is alone and then we kill him, what have we really accomplished? We can leave now, go up river and start over. We can build a new version of our old life. There is nothing here for us, Tomek. Uncle is dead, Hawkins is dead and..."

Drake's end point was interrupted by the loud sound of static and a short screech filling the air. The voice coming from the speakers strewn throughout the entire property of Lucky Trail was not familiar to them other than the one time they had heard it in the past. It was not that Father Niko had an overly recognizable sound. However it was his cadence that made them aware of exactly who was broadcasting the message.

"Yea though I walk through the shadow of death I fear no evil, come say hello, twins. Your sister and I have been expecting you."

The words hit them both as if a bear had pounced upon them. Was the mayor telling the truth they wondered? But if Annette was really working with Father Niko the whole time, why were the angels trying to kill her? If Annette was here with Niko then maybe her plan was for them to be a part of Lucky Trail. Did their older sister, who was now the sheriff want them to serve as part of Niko's kids? It was, after all, a place meant to save the lost innocence of troubled kids. And there certainly was no more troubled kids than Tomek and Drake Henderson. So many questions, so many lies and only one way to find out the truth.

Tomek started walking briskly towards the large group of buildings near the front of the area where the driveway ended. The square brick open-sided pavilion-type structures looked more like barracks than anything else and the twins found them empty as well. Rows upon rows of bunk beds were neatly made as if they had never seen a night of sleep in their existence. Passing the four sets of empty barracks each one of them as large and as empty as the last Drake followed his brother and matched his briskly-paced walk. Each step made purposely and with enough aggressiveness to let Drake know that nothing he said would stop his twin brother at this point.

Drake followed in tow, crossbow fully cocked with a bolt upon the rail. Tomek removed an arrow from his back quiver and nocked it against the string as they reached the front stone steps of the chapel. On any other occasion they may have noticed the detailed beauty that was present in the buildings architecture, but not now, not today.

As they began opening the large heavy wooden doors atop the steps, the twins were hit with the overpowering smell of something rotting. The musty scent seemed to be emanating from the nave area as they pushed forward into the building. Standing at the back of the cathedral they looked forward to the altar where Father Niko stood in the same place just as he had been on the video.

The pews were full of young boys all of whom appeared to be to between the ages of ten and eighteen. The twins stood there, looking down each pew row as they walked forward. Their weapons drawn and aimed toward the priest who had yet to acknowledge their presence. Father Niko just stood there looking forward at the approaching brothers remaining silent.

Once reaching the altar they stood a mere twelve feet from Niko. In passing by every pew, they confirmed each row held the same as the last. The rows were full, full of young boys dressed in the same green polo style-shirt as both Drake and Tomek. The same one they had put on in the guard shack. Looking behind them, they saw again each row full, full of young boys lying on their backs without shoes or socks upon their feet. Every single row was full, full of young boys and men in what Father Niko intended to be their final resting place.

They were no longer boys, they were now bodies. Not a single one of them was alive. The source of the foul smell was now evident. Each one of them had drinketh from the cup of God. The cup that Father Niko now held out in his hands offering to the twins.

The twins stood there among hundreds of dead bodies and felt a presence among them that was greater than any they had before. Uncle had taken his own life just like the rows and rows of Niko's kids before them.

For the first time in many years Tomek and Drake felt, afraid.

25 NIKO

"What have you done?" Drake asked aiming the crossbow at Niko with the safety off and his finger on the metal trigger.

"I have done nothing, they have all chosen to follow their own path into glory," Father Niko replied. "And now they sit at the right hand of the Almighty in His kingdom of everlasting joy. You see they have been saved. Have you?" Father Niko asked the twins who still both had their weapons drawn and aimed upon him.

"The only one needing to be saved around here is you," Tomek threatened.

"Be that as it may child, I shall join my boys in Heaven. Might my angels be there as well?" Father Niko asked.

"Your thug-ass angel's wings got clipped all right. And they definitely have gone somewhere. But I can downright tell you it wasn't Heaven. Straight to Hell for that batch of demons. Now I hope you are ready to join them," Drake said.

"Timothy four my son, Timothy four," Niko said disregarding the twins threats.

"Why are crazy old men always calling me their son? I ain't your son, and the last two guys that made that mistake are both dead!" Tomek replied referencing the old sheriff and the mayor.

"So the drugs, all this time were for this?" Drake asked.

"Timothy four my son, Timothy four," Niko said disregarding the twin's threats again.

"You killed all these children you sick demon and for what? So you can claim righteousness while standing here to quote a book of fairy tales? Where is my sister?" Tomek was now yelling at Niko.

"Timothy four my son, Timothy four," Niko repeated.

"I hope you are ready to learn just how wrong you are about the afterlife." Drake said as he squeezed the grip of the crossbow readying it for the fire position.

Father Niko raised the gold-plated chalice in the air and began preaching from the fourth chapter of the book Timothy. "For I am already being poured out like a drink offering, and the time has come for my departure. I have fought the good fight, I have finished the race, I have kept the faith."

"There is no virtue in faith, look what it has done to these kids. You have destroyed their souls," Drake said challenging the priest.

"They have chosen their destiny and so must you," Father Niko replied.

"If one truly has a destiny, it cannot be chosen. Cause if you choose it, then by definition it is not actually a destiny. If there is a Hell I hope you rot in it for eternity," Tomek said as he kept the bowstring tight against his fingers waiting for Father Niko to make his next move.

Both twins wanted him dead, yet for some reason they hesitated on sending him to Hell right there upon the altar. Perhaps it was the slight respect that they had for the church in general that kept them from sending an arrow into his body. Killing a priest upon the altar no matter how wicked he may be appeared to be troublesome, even for the likes of Tomek and Drake. The moment seemed as if it lasted for hours yet only minutes had passed.

The tension in his shoulders and back muscles would soon force Tomek to either shoot or let down the string. Just as he began to let down the string, Niko took as step toward them and said,

"Good bye for now twins, I shall now taketh the seat amongst my angels and children of God."

Father Niko raised the chalice to his lips and swallowed the remaining contents of the cup. Dropping to his knees he began to pray in a tongue that was unrecognizable to both Drake and Tomek. It was not English nor even Latin which he was known to speak from time to time. The last words he spoke seemed to be cut off by his falling forward off the front three steps where he landed face down, dead like the children that drank from the very same cup before him.

There was no sound in the large cathedral. The silence of the room's occupants had been caused by an overly lethal dose of potassium cyanide mixed into the sacramental wine. As it turned out, the blood of Christ was to blame for the quick deaths of every lifeless body inside Niko's house of God. Tomek and Drake stood there taking it all in. Wondering how their small, lonely woodland way of life and survival had led them to the grandiose situation of both life and death that was now before them.

Looking at each other, they both simply shrugged and remembered clearly what Uncle had preached to them many a time.

All things live and all things die.

Walking back towards the front door, they stopped at each row. Looking over the boys, dressed the same as them. Most with the same skin color as them. They were not openly praying, but it was as if they both felt that some show of respect was appropriate. They all looked peaceful as if they had just fallen asleep. The twins knew after watching Father Niko succumb to the sacrament that there was no way each child laid there on his own. Niko must of placed them there post mortem. It would have been a lot of work but perhaps the angels were still around at that point to assist.

"What now?" Tomek said questioning Drake as to their future plans.

"I don't know, I just don't know anymore," Drake replied.

"I say we go find her, get the hell out of this place and make a new life together." Tomek suggested talking about his sister Sheriff Henderson.

Drake sighed and turned to look back at the cathedral full of death. Taking in the gravity of the situation he remained confused on what their next action should be. Turning back he put his arm around his brother as they began walking out of the building as they reached the front door they stopped. Drake then sighed again and looked at his brother,

"If you want to go find her, then go. I support you, but I can't. I just can't," Drake explained.

"Where you go, I go," Tomek said showing solidarity to his brother.

"Good then, let's go home," Drake replied.

Upon pushing the large wooden doors to the building open, Tomek stood on the front steps and noticed strange red dots had appeared on his chest. This made Tomek curiously look up into the parking area as Drake had simultaneously noticed the exact same dot upon his torso.

Standing there, with assault rifles drawn were two Michigan State Police SWAT Troopers. The laser sights of their AR-15 tactical weapons projected forward and illumined the chests of both twins. The reticules upon their bodies were a clear indication that only one of two things was going to happen. If they did not surrender they would be finding out if Father Niko was correct in regards to the possibility of a so-called afterlife.

Dropping their weapons, the decision was made to live, to survive. The two Troopers fully decked out in tactical ballistic gear and shields slowly moved forward ordering the twins to the ground. Their orders fell upon deaf ears as neither Tomek or Drake complied. They just stood there looking at the two approaching them unsure of exactly what was happening.

The lead Trooper reached up lifting the drop down visor affixed to his riot helmet exposing his face and again ordered them to the ground. This time the command was well received and both Tomek and Drake slumped to their knees with their hands behind their backs.

The second SWAT officer approached them and like the other raised the helmet's visor.

"Hello boys," Sheriff Henderson said causing them both to look up at the surprise of hearing Annette's voice. They were happy to see her, however they sincerely wished that Trooper Common was not present for the family reunion as well. However after his catching of Henderson from her improvised rope fail she felt he deserved to be there as well.

The large doors of the church remained propped open as Trooper Common glanced inside to the true horror that was upon them all.

"Sheriff, you need to see this," He said asking Henderson to join him inside.

Trooper Common secured Drake's hands in thick plastic zip tie restraints as Henderson did the same to Tomek. Lifting both the boys up and walking them back into the chapel, Henderson observed what lay before them. Letting go of Tomek she walked up the middle of the aisle looking row by row at the numerous empty souls that filled the room.

Looking back at her brothers, emotion took over and her eyes began filling with both tears and hate. Wiping away the pain she looked at them both once more and asked,

"What have you done?"

Will Tomek and Drake be held responsible for Father Niko's Master Plan?

Or

Will Sheriff Henderson believe they had nothing to do with it and finally get the family she has so longed for all these years.

Find out when the Twins story concludes in book number 3.

To purchase *Twins of Prey III ~ Ascension*: Click the link below.

CLICK HERE to Start Reading Twins of Prey III

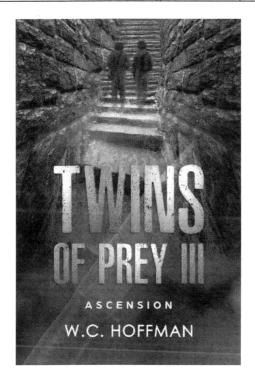

Join My "New Release" Mailing List

Want to stay up to date with W.C. Hoffman? All members receive a FREE SHORT STORY and discounted prices on future books.

https://wchoffman.weebly.com

Made in the USA
Columbia, SC
22 February 2023

12833471R00109